RAVENHART

Paul Mortimer

To Jo

who's vision, encouragement and enthusiasm

has given life to so many ideas.

Chapter 1

'LOOKS like a mugging gone wrong chief.'

'Hmm.' Jackson grunted and took another bite out of the hamburger he'd grabbed on his way to the scene. Rubbish swirled round the alley as a gust swept in off the main street. Traffic and a few pedestrians streamed by at the end; people oblivious of a murder scene. Jackson screwed up the bag, tossed it aside and wiped his mouth with his raincoat sleeve. 'Do we know how he died?'

'Nope. There's no wounds whatever,' said McClure. 'I'm guessing maybe he banged his head hard when he hit the ground.'

Jackson looked at the sergeant, his face expressionless. 'So you solved it already then Sergeant. Nice job, guess I'll just get back to the warmth of the office then.'

McClure shrugged his shoulders and thought better of a reply.

Jackson knelt down by the body and went through the pockets. 'He's been picked clean that's for sure, not a cent on him. Zip.' Another gust cut down the alley, but this time with an edge to it and Jackson sunk deeper into his coat. Something caught his eye. 'Well, will you look at this.' He was holding up an arm and dangling from the sleeve of the overcoat was a stiff label and a price ticket.

'Dressed to kill, eh chief?' McClure chuckled at his own joke. No-one else did. 'When does the pathologist get down here?' he said to no-one in particular. There was no answer. A couple of police photographers kept lighting up the scene with their flash guns. Other officers were carefully trawling through debris in the alley.

Jackson went back to the tape at the entrance, patted his pockets looking for his cigarettes. Then remembered he was supposed to be giving up. 'Give me a cigarette someone.'

'Sir?'

'Don't even go there McClure, just give me one.' He clicked his fingers, took the cigarette and his Sergeant gave him a light.

'Kinda odd chief. That new coat.'

'Hmm.' What Jackson found even stranger was

that there was nothing in any of the pockets. Under the new wool coat, the victim was wearing a rather odd leather jerkin and black trousers. He could accept a missing wallet, but there was no loose change. Not even a screwed up tissue in his pants. He drew long and hard and blew the smoke up into the air.

'What we got then?'

Jackson turned round. He'd known Art Williams a long time. He stood there with his well-worn black leather bag. He called it his tool kit. 'He's down there, can't miss him.'

'What we got?'

'Male, white, dead.'

'Injuries?'

'Nothing visible for sure, but go easy Art. It's a strange one.'

'The pathologist raised an eyebrow.

Jackson shrugged. 'We don't want too much disturbed just now. Until forensics have finished up. The guy's wearing a new coat. I mean really new, with the labels still on and all.' Art grunted and walked off to the end of the alley, now lit with the lamps set up by forensics.

At 48 with one marriage and numerous relationships trailing in his wake, Jackson was effectively wedded to the police department. He'd joined the force on leaving college and had always worked out of Portland's Middle Street building. He had been with the Patrol and Traffic units before switching to CID at the age of 27. He was sharp, taciturn, thorough and, being a Maine boy, had a stream of contacts by the age of 23 that had detectives turning to him for help. Becoming one himself was only a matter of time. And now he headed up the *Crime Against People Division*, one of the six teams within the CID. Jackson had seen just about everything people do to other people. He was on the cusp of seeing something completely new.

'I thought you were giving those things up?' said Art.

'Yeah well, gotta keep warm somehow.' Jackson barked a short laugh. It was barely November and already the Portland nights were getting cold. According to the news, it was supposed to drop below freezing at the weekend.

'Well, there's not much I can do here. As you said, no outward signs of anything. Looks like the John just fell into a permanent sleep back there.'

'Yeah. When we finished up here I'll give you a call and let you know he's on his way to you.'

'Thanks Jackson. Take care of yourself.'

Jackson was aware of McClure at his shoulder. At 24 he was almost everything Jackson wasn't; quick sense of humour, sometimes a bit mouthy, had several girls in tow and gregarious. But he was also a good cop. Jackson liked him for his thoroughness and his ability to chase things down. 'We finished here chief?'

Jackson looked at his watch. Still not yet 8 am. 'Guess there's no point staying here any longer. Let's get back downtown and start making some calls.'

As they left the alley Jackson suddenly felt uncomfortable. Like he was being watched. He rolled his shoulders as they headed back to the car, but it wouldn't pass. As he stood by the passenger door, hand on the handle, he took a casual look around. He saw a man staring at him intently from the sidewalk across St Lawrence Street. Jackson's swept his gaze past him, but took in the details. Just over six feet, longish black hair, on the skinny side, not much more than 190 pounds. 'Just start up the engine but don't move yet.' He pulled out his cell phone, one-shot a number out of his contacts list. 'Bob, you still down in the alley with your camera boys? I want you to do me a favour. There's a guy on the sidewalk opposite the alley entrance. Sneak me a shot of him will you? Cheers. Ok let's go, McClure.'

The sergeant edged out into the traffic and headed back to the department. 'What's that about chief?'

'Someone taking a lot of interest in what's going on back there. I found it unnerving.'

McClure looked at him out of the corner of his eye. 'Chief?'

The rest of the trip back to the Middle Street station passed in silence. Jackson was brooding. Barely an hour into the case, and already he was finding it unsettling.

There was something about Mr Pilkington that didn't fit. He had been at the Harbor View hotel for three weeks. Ryan was on reception when he arrived. The guest's manner wasn't abrupt or uncivil, but he didn't connect. As if Ryan was just part of a function. Mr Pilkington certainly dressed smart enough; after all, the harbour front hotel was not one of the cut-price efforts buried back in the city. No, Mr Pilkington was a puzzle. And now here he was striding — almost loping; thought Ryan — across reception to his desk.

'Morning, Mr Pilkington. You've been out early.' It was still not yet 9 am.

'My key please.'

There it was again, a politeness but almost on the edge of rudeness. Ryan turned, lifted the key off the board. Turned back and held it out, smiling. Mr Pilkington took it without a word and headed for the stairs. Always the stairs, never the lift. 'An odd bird,' said Ryan quietly. 'He doesn't drive, doesn't use a credit card, doesn't have a cell phone. That guy isn't American!' Then it struck him: Mr Pilkington never smiled. Not once. Not ever. He didn't smile with his mouth. He didn't smile with his eyes. He was, decided Ryan, a very cold man. But oddly for that, he felt there was no aura of danger or menace about him. He just didn't fit.

Crolin was brooding. Alarmed, but brooding. He hadn't meant to kill him. He had just wanted to reason with him, make him see sense. Talk him round then take him back. Crolin was surprised by the fierceness of the argument that followed. He was surprised by his own over-reaction, the strength of his response. And so death was inevitable. Now here he was. Trapped. He knew with a cold certainly that a hunt for him would now begin.

There was a gentle knock on the door. Mr Pilkington opened it and took the breakfast tray from the waiter.

'Thank you sir.'

He said nothing, carried the tray across his room and put it on the coffee table. Then he went to the window. From the fifth floor the view across Portland Harbor front was spectacular. It was a clear

sharp morning, giving the water a metallic sheen.
Around its edges were the old dock piers and rough
structures mixed with some of Portland's impressive,
famous, red brick buildings. Mr Pilkington took none
of this in. His mind was methodically sifting through
the last three days. Stitching together strands of
information he had gathered as he had tracked both
his targets. Now the whole thing had exploded. A
shadow quickly passed across his face. Mr
Pilkington faced a difficult decision. Then he thought
about Crolin. He was in big trouble. Over-reached
himself, got himself trapped. There was certainly no
way back for him just now. Ryan would have been
surprised; Mr Pilkington smiled.

Jackson sat at his desk staring out of the
window. There wasn't much of a view. Just a jumble
of buildings cluttered in the frame. 'Do me a favour
McClure. Go get me a large coffee from Stephanie's.
I need something decent, not the crap we got here.'
'Sure chief.'
The call had come at 6 am, but Jackson was
already up. A body in an alley off St Lawrence Street

and Doug Blain had just checked out of his shift. So Jackson made the trip downtown, picking up his sergeant on the way. It had been found by a cleaner putting garbage out in the alley. Being head of the *Crime Against Persons* section didn't mean Jackson was chasing homicides every day. After all Portland wasn't exactly one of America's crime hotbed cities. There were rarely more than 25 murders in any one year and around 3,000 recorded violent crimes. But it was still enough to keep Jackson and his team busy. Indeed there was only one on-going murder investigation on their books just now; the body of a woman had been found in July, dumped just off Maine Turnpike at Riverton.

The investigation had ground to halt. They didn't even know if she was local. So the whole thing was just hanging in the air with no place to go. It agitated Jackson. He liked things cleaned up, but was at a loss. Now here he had another potential mystery victim on his hands.

McClure came in carrying two large coffees in the Stephanie's blue and black styrofoam cups. He set them down on Jackson's table and fished a bag of cookies out of his jacket pocket.

'That's bad.'

'No worries chief, I can manage them. So what's the deal today?'

Jackson popped the lid off his mug. Steam and coffee smells whirled into the air. He reached into the bag and pulled out a double choc-chip, took a bite and leant back in his chair.

'We'll give Art until midday and then hassle him over the *post mortem*. See what we got. When the photos are in I want you to get the victim's mug shot out to the divisions. See if we can get an ID this time.'

'What about the guy on the sidewalk?'

'I don't want to rush that out.'

'No?'

'Gotta hunch about him. Just want to keep it under wraps for now while we make some inquiries. I want you to run him through our database first. Let's see if we pull anything up.'

'So we just sit and wait.' McClure put his feet up on the desk.

Jackson looked at him. 'Not you, Sergeant. I

want you out asking questions round the area back there. See if anything was seen or heard.'

'What about his coat?'

'Yeah I've been thinking about that. Let me make a call.' He rang through to the Maine State Police crime lab. 'Give me Bob Webber. It's Jackson here.

Hiya, Bob. Nope, not after stuff yet, just want to check that you got close ups of the coat, tabs and label the John was wearing yet? Good. Appreciate it if you could get those to me fast, along with a mug shot.'

'And?' McClure waited as Jackson replaced the receiver.

'And nothing. Just go talk to some people. Now.'

McClure fished his coffee mug lid out the bin, snapped it on and left the office.

Jackson picked up his cell phone. 'Hi, Trish. I need a favour. Can you meet 10.30 at Steph's? Excellent!' He sipped his coffee and tried to work out what was worrying him about this case. Jackson was not a premonitions man. He was a down-to-earth

Portland boy who took things at face value. Things outside facts and reasoning were not part of his baggage, either on police work or in his private life, but he was niggled. There was a bad feeling stirring in his gut and it made him uncomfortable.

Sam McClure was not having much success. He had spoken to four people living near the murder scene and got nowhere. He'd also been confronted by several unanswered doors. The morning was bright, but the wind cold. Being outside wasn't comfortable. He took another walk down the alley. Just to take in the scene. He was sure forensics had been thorough. New litter spiralled in the gusts of wind. All the old stuff had been taken away for examination earlier that morning. Canyon walls stretched up either side of him dark as they always were. This was a place the sun never reached. One had a metal fire escape climbing away up the block. He decided to check it out. Three floors up he found it. There, shining against the black iron floor, was a small silver object. McClure fished in his coat and brought out a plastic bag. Scooped it up and examined it. 'Hmmm. Interesting. The boys missed that one.'

It looked like a button or badge. It was about the size of a quarter, but had a very odd picture on one side. It most certainly wasn't George Washington. More like some creature. McClure pocketed the badge and continued his search up the escape. Ten minutes later he was down in the alley and heading back towards his car. He heard someone shouting him as he emerged from the alley.

'Mister, mister!'

McClure turned to see a large woman approaching. He waited. She was breathing heavily as she stopped and set down two large shopping bags. 'You know what went on here last night?' she gasped out.

'Well, that depends.'

'On what?'

'Who's asking.'

'You a cop or something?'

'Are you?' Then he smiled and she burst out laughing.

'Man you're just too smart for your own good. I live across the road,' she pointed to the buildings on St Lawrence Street, 'and I just saw the cops here this morning and wondered what was happening.'

'Well, ma'am we just have an issue here to clear up. Where do you live?'

'Over there,' she pointed again. 'Number 1756E, up on the third floor. Been there 16 years now and this is a good neighbourhood. So why all the cops?'

He ignored the question. 'Did you hear anything last night or this morning?'

'You mean apart from traffic and the TV?'

He narrowed his eyes.

'Yup, you're a cop.'

'So, anything unusual?'

'I guess. I'm a sound sleeper mister, but that racket sure as hell woke me up.'

In the back of his mind McClure was wondering why the others he talked to hadn't heard a 'hell of a racket.' But then people didn't like to get involved.

'Go on.'

'There was shouting and hollerin'. It woke me up like I said.'

'What time would that be?'

'It was 2.42. Those damn digital clock lights are so bright. I mean bright. Green glowing like something watching you while you sleep.'

'Go on.'

'Well, like I said; there was this yelling so I got up and looked outta the window. There was a guy chasing another down the street, shouting after him. The first one cut up the alley over there, the other followed him.'

'Then what?'

'It went kinda quiet. I watched for a good while. Maybe 30 minutes but neither of them came out. So I went back to bed.'

'Did you get a good look at either of them.'

She just gave him a look.

'I know. It was dark. But with the lights you must have got some sort of description for me.'

'The second fella was big. I don't mean fat. I mean big. He stood tall. Way over six feet and man the width of his shoulders. I bet he could hug me good.' She chuckled.

'What about the guy he was chasing?'

'All I can say is he was smaller. He moved fast.'

'Right ...,' McClure was suddenly aware he didn't know her name. He flashed his ID at her and asked.

'Beth Donald.'

'Ok Beth, here's what's going to happen. I'm going to get someone to bring you down to the station this afternoon to make a statement.'

Her eyes popped wide.

'It's nothing for you to worry about Beth. We just need to gather all the information we can.'

'What's happened?'

'We found a body in the alley.'

Her hand shot to her mouth.

'There's nothing to worry about.' He could almost read her thoughts.

'It isn't a maniac killer on the loose Beth. This is a one-off incident and we just need info to help us. What you've seen can help us put the pieces together.'

She nodded her head.

'So is it ok if I send a car round for you at 2.30?'

'Yes, sir.'

'Right here's my card.' He tapped it. 'That's my number right there. Direct line. Call me if you remember anything else meantime. Otherwise, I'll see you later.'

'Yes, sir.'

'Thanks for your help Beth.' He touched her arm. Then watched her as she crossed the road to her apartment.

At last! A couple of pieces of puzzle. He sat in the car, wrote up a few notes in his book, fired up the engine and started to head back to the station. Then a thought struck him. Tucking his cell phone between his shoulder and ear he waited while the number rang out. 'Hey Lisa, you free for few minutes, I need a favour? Cool be there in five.' He turned up a side street and worked his way back to *Portland Museum of Art* off High Street. Which, ironically, was just a couple of blocks away from the murder scene.

Chapter 2

'SO what do you think?'

'Can I take it out the bag?'

He shook his head. Then watched as yet again she tucked her hair behind one ear. Peered closely at the badge, button, coin, whatever.

'Dinner tonight?'

'History,' said Lisa without looking up.

'Well, I guess that's what you specialise in.'

'You want me to help you with this? Or are you trying to get something back on track?'

'Maybe both,' he ventured. Then she looked up. Brown eyes regarding him steadily. He barely stopped himself from flinching. 'Ok, ok.' He held up his hands'.

'Sam. We had a good thing going last year and you screwed it up. Right?'

'Right.'

She looked back at the object. 'So what time you picking me up?'

''Bout eight?'

'Make it eight.'

'Cool. So what do you reckon then?'

'Never seen anything like it.'

'What's the picture on it?'

'Well, Sam it's odd. To me it looks like something from mythology, but I'm not so hot on that. Can I keep it for a while?'

'No chance! The chief would probably skin me if he even knew I'd brought it here first instead of sending it to the lab.'

'Right. Give me a second.'

He watched her as she swayed out the room. Thinking back to the fun times they'd had last year. Then remembering why it all hit the buffers and wondering if he'd been wise to ask her out again. McClure shrugged his shoulders and peered into some of the glass cabinets in the storeroom. Lumps of rock, pottery and strangely painted pieces. Not to his taste.

Lisa came back with a camera, set a spotlight over the object and took several photos of both sides. 'There.' She handed him the bag.

'So at eight then. Meet you at *Caltronio's*?'

'Sounds good to me.'

He wasn't sure whether to peck her on the cheek or not. He smiled warmly and left.

Jackson looked irritably at his watch. Where the hell had McClure got to. It was just gone 10.00 and things should be kicking off soon. He rang the front desk. 'Anyone seen McClure sneak in the building yet? Well, if you see him make sure he gets his ass up here fast.' Jackson was not the most patient of men. He wanted to start things running properly. Hated standing on the starting line. The phone rang. 'Sure I'll come up.'

Brett Rotsko was at his desk. The usual pile of paperwork on one side. He wasn't a Maine man, joining the force ten years ago from Cincinnati. His background was impressive, from a cop's point of view anyway. Rotsko was a cop's cop and that's what probably stopped him getting any higher than Assistant Police Chief. Normally, a man headed for the very top would have moved on some years ago. Brett was resigned to the fact that he'd got as far as he was going to. It was not for want of trying. He had

put in for a couple of Chief of Police posts but didn't
make either of them. After that he gave up. He liked
Portland and was happy to see his career out here.
At 52 that wasn't far down the track.

In Cincinnati he had been instrumental in
breaking down two major crime operations. One was
a drugs cartel linked to South America. Rotsko had
set the gang up with a now legendary sting, but had
got shot in the final raid and was laid up for six
months.

The second marker he had laid down, the one
which probably sealed his promotion and move to
Portland, was more sobering. He had uncovered
corruption in one of the divisions and it had been a
painful investigation. It involved protection and
backhanders. Towards the end, Rotsko discovered
that his long-time buddy was caught up in it and had
to stand aside while the hammer dropped. But his
tenacity had nailed the case. He had impressed the
people at Portland enough to land the assistant's
job.

Jackson liked him. Rotsko was straight talking,
hated the admin side of his job and was always

trying to poke in on investigations. Those smart enough to realise how good he was welcomed the interference. Jackson was one of them. 'Hey, Brett, how's the pen-work going?' Jackson sat on the sofa and grinned as Rotsko huffed.

'You know me. Love all that stuff. Don't fancy a promotion do you, switching roles?'

Jackson laughed. 'Screw that.'

'So what's this that turned up last night?'

Jackson laughed again. 'Man you must be bored to be poking your nose that quick into my case.'

'You know me. Just interested. Coffee?' The one thing Jackson did envy about Rotsko's job was the fact he always had a pot on the go in his office. He didn't wait for an answer and poured a mug for each of them.

'To be straight, Brett there's not much to tell just now. The body of some John has turned up in an alley off St Lawrence Street. We only got to him a coupla hours ago so still waiting for the first wave of stuff to come back from the lab. Art should also have something for us this afternoon.'

'And?'

Jackson raised an eye. 'You're too smart for your own good.' He still never failed to be surprised at how quickly Rotsko could pick up on the unsaid.

'Come on Jackson, out with it.'

'Well, the odd thing was how the guy was dressed. His top coat was brand new.'

'Nothing strange in that.'

'There is when the label and price tag are still dangling on it. Then underneath was some old leather jerkin.'

'Oh?'

'Yeah, exactly. I sent McClure out to talk to people in the neighbourhood, but he ain't got back yet.'

'Champing at the bit Jackson? Don't worry it'll soon all kick off. Just keep me in the loop. Out of interest you understand. Life's a bit tedious round here just now.' He swept his arm round his office. Then he looked at Jackson. Didn't miss the quick frown. 'Something else?'

'Well, I'm not sure Brett. I've got an odd feeling about this. Not a comfortable one either.'

'What's kicked that off?'

'Nothing I can put my finger on. There's something worrying away inside me about it.' He decided not to tell him about the guy on the pavement. He'd already said too much. Stepping into stuff outside his comfort zone. 'Anyway, I need to see if McClure's got back. Catch you later.' Jackson strode briskly out the office.

Rotsko watch him go. He was slightly puzzled.

Jackson remembered his meeting with Trish. 'Damn!' He stopped off at the front counter on his way out. 'If McClure finally decides to turn up tell him I'll be back in about 20 minutes.'

Stephanie's was pretty full, but then they did make the best coffee and pastries in town. At least Jackson thought so. The place looked like someone's front room, only much bigger. There were numerous large, grey-brown cracked leather sofas and chairs dotted about. Mirrors and pictures with gilt frames, old fashioned lamps and lights, a variety of wooden tables and chairs scattered about giving the whole place a cosy feeling. Certainly not one of your franchised, same-look coffee-chain outfits. The coffee bar ran down one side with a brass foot-rail and high stools. Behind it a number of machines were hissing and spitting. Dotted between them were shelves of coffee jars. Jackson believed there wasn't a coffee anywhere in the world that you wouldn't find up there! A rack of newspapers stood just inside the door and the air was filled with the hum of quiet chatter and coffee. Jackson could quite happily waste a day away in here.

He spotted Trish sitting in a large soft chair, with two mugs of coffee on the table in front of her. She waved briefly as he caught her eye.
Trish Longton was dressed immaculately, as usual. Her dark hair was cut into a neat bob. She wore a simple, startlingly white pencil skirt and champagne-coloured silk blouse. The only pieces of jewellery were a thin gold chain round her neck and a slim gold bangle on her left wrist. No watch, no rings.

'Hello Jackson.'

He bent down and kissed her on the cheek, sat and picked up his coffee. 'Thanks Trish.'

She smiled and regarded him steadily with her

grey eyes. He had often wondered about asking her out, but with his track record, he didn't want to ruin their four-year-long close friendship. She found that frustrating, but had decided she would pick her moment.

'So how can I help? Must be important for such a quick meeting.'

Jackson frowned. 'It's a tricky one Trish. In a way I'm giving you a bit of a heads up because I've got a feeling about this one that niggles at me.'

'Go on.'

'A guy was found in an alley off St Lawrence Street this morning. Deceased. I'm waiting for photos and the first raft of info back from forensics. Shouldn't be long. Art will have something for me this afternoon.'

Trish was intrigued. This case was barely out of the blocks yet. She found it vaguely disturbing that the detective seemed to be a bit perplexed so early in to the case. 'Not known you to get spooked before Jackson. What's triggered that off?'

'Well, I don't want to go into details just now. Be best if you had an open mind to be honest.'

As vice president of marketing and planning at Maine Medical Centre and a senior board member of Portland Regional Chamber, Trish Longton was well connected in the community. She was also highly analytical and when Jackson couldn't see a way out of the woods, Trish always helped steer him through. They were a good team when heavy thinking was needed and he valued that. If Jackson's seniors knew of his sounding board, they never let on; in the end he got results. Well, most of the time; the July body was still an open case and even Trish hadn't helped him get an angle on that one.

'So you're just booking in a slot then.' She smiled.

'That sounds bad when you put it like that. Like I'm using you.'

'And aren't you?' She laughed at his obvious discomfort. Reached across, touched him lightly on his hand. 'Its fine Jackson, you know I love this clandestine detective work. Makes my real work more bearable. So when are you going to give me something to go on?'

'It depends what turns up later today. Maybe I'll

give you a call tomorrow.'

She toyed with the idea of suggesting dinner, then thought better of it. Jackson was way too preoccupied just now. That'll keep. 'Ok. Not a problem.'

'Thanks for the coffee Trish. You know I value having you off patch to talk this stuff out of my head. Just want to make sure you're up for this one.'

'Of course!' She watched him stride out of Steph's and smiled to herself.

As he walked back through the door he saw McClure at his desk, talking on the phone. 'Sorry to interrupt you Sergeant, but you got anything interesting to say to me?'

'Catch you later.' McClure hung up. He filled Jackson in on his talk with people in the neighbourhood and what Beth Donald had seen.

'So we got one woman woken up in the early hours from the racket in the alley and a bunch of others who heard nothing?'

''Bout the size of it.'

'Well, we need to talk to them again. Best if

you go back this evening and catch others who've been out during the day.'

'This evening? I gotta a date chief!'

'Not my problem, McClure.' At least it was the first breakthrough. Jackson felt the handbrake had finally been taken off the investigation. He knew for sure that Beth Donald wasn't the only one who heard what kicked off. And more importantly, someone else may be able to add to the ID. Jackson reached for the phone.

'There's something else chief.'

He put the phone down. McClure laid the small plastic bag on the desk in front of the detective. Jackson looked at it and looked back up at McClure. He raised an eyebrow inviting an explanation.

'Well I decided to have another poke around in the alley. Just in case forensics missed anything.'

Jackson looked back at the bag. 'You found this on the ground? After they picked the place clean?'

'Nope. I checked up the fire escape. Found it three floors up, just lying there.'

'You reckon those guys missed it?'

'I'm guessing they didn't even climb up there.'

'Possibly.' Jackson picked up the bag. Squinted at the object. Turned the bag over. Squinted again.

'Odd. Looks like some badge or button.'

'Could be a foreign coin,' ventured McClure.

'Hmm. I'll get it down to the lab for prints. But we really need some sort of expert to look at this. Fast.'

McClure glanced down at his feet.

'McClure?'

'Well, I figured as I was already in the neighbourhood I'd pop in and see Lisa Schwark at the museum.'

Jackson frowned. 'Thought you two gone you're separate ways. What did you want to see her for?' He already knew the answer.

'My thinking was that as she's a bit of an expert in old artefacts and stuff it wouldn't hurt to show her.'

'Please tell me it stayed in the bag.'

'It stayed in the bag.'

'What did she make of it?'

'Said she'd never seen anything like it. Took a bunch of photos and is going to get back to me.'

'I should haul your ass for that McClure. Wrong route, but on this occasion right call.'

McClure left the office wondering if he'd been balled out or praised. 'Probably both,' he muttered.

Mr Pilkington left his hotel shortly after eleven. He put his keys on the reception desk without comment. Ryan picked them up and watched the guest leave in that unusual loping stride. Time was now critical. The death had suddenly fast-forwarded his agenda. The Gatetrap was still active for another five days, but that wasn't his immediate concern. He waved down a cab. 'I need to get out to St Lawrence Street.'

'You got an address there?'

'I'll tell you where to drop me off.'

'Ok boss. Getting cold now. Wonder what sort of winter will hit us this year.'

Mr Pilkington said nothing. The rest of the journey passed in silence.

'Here we are. Where do you want me to stop?'

'Up near the top by Monument Street junction.'

Mr Pilkington paid him and watched the cab drive off before doubling back down the road. He cut into the alley where the body had been found. It had to be here somewhere. He summoned up all his mental energy.

The phone made Jackson jump. He snatched the receiver. 'Yes? 'Hi Bob. Right … see you in about ten minutes.' The phone went dead. Jackson stared at the receiver, his mind working hard.

'What is it chief?'

'Bob says they got the photos for us.'

'Good! Courier shouldn't be long then.'

'They're not coming by courier. Bob's bringing them himself. He said there's something really strange showed up and doesn't want anyone else to see them just yet.'

With 18 years behind him, Bob Webber had seen everything. Or so he thought. Forensics had fascinated him from the age of 14. After that it was all he was ever going to do. On leaving high school he went to Pennsylvania State University where he completed a degree in Forensic Science. His first job was down in Boston. It was a wrench leaving his family and friends at just outside Portland so when the chance of promotion came with a post at Portland lab he grabbed it fast. Then he met Faye and life followed an almost perfect path from there. He had a job he loved, lived in the city he loved, shared a home with a woman he loved — they passed on the marriage bit — and had a great group of friends.

His line of work required a thoroughness that was second nature. It was detective work in its own way as he teased out information hidden by all kinds of objects and scenes. Bob was renowned as a stickler which irked some of his younger colleagues at times. But he got results. So when he was first shown the two photos from that morning by Vern he figured he'd got something wrong and sent him back to try again. Vern started to argue, thought better of it and went back to his computer. He rang Bob twenty minutes later.

'No mistake Bob.'

He went down to Vern's office, sat himself at

the computer and ran the digital programme again. Stared at the screen. Totally perplexed.

'Is this a programme bug, Vern?'

''Fraid not. That's what the camera saw this morning. Sure beats the hell out of me.'

'You tell nobody about this. Not a soul until I've spoken to Jackson. He'll decide where we take it from there. Got that?'

'Sure. But what do you think?'

'I don't know what to think,' he said, almost to himself. 'That is totally weird. But logic dictates there must be an answer.' He transferred the images to a pen drive. Put it in his pocket.

'Just for now you put that folder in an extremely secure place on your computer and lock it up with a password. I don't want anyone else near that.'

'No probs.'

Jackson's door was never shut. Bob walked in, glanced at McClure and went over to Jackson's desk. He sat down. The detective raised his eyebrows.

'So what's so important that I get a personal visit, Bob?'

He chucked an envelope in front of him. 'First you better take a look at those.'

Jackson opened it. Took out a small bundle of about ten prints and sifted through them. They were pictures of the victim, mostly close ups. He looked like he was asleep. A long thin face, unmarked. Blond hair, almost shoulder length.

'The other photos?'

'Maybe you need to get those ones sent out.' He gave an almost imperceptible nod toward the sergeant.

Jackson caught his drift. 'McClure,' he held out the photos. 'You know what to do with those.' As he left the room Jackson got up, went over and shut the door.

'So?'

'The dude on the sidewalk, I got Vernon to fire off some shots. These are what he got.' He produced another envelope and took out one picture. 'He reckons he fired off about ten shots. I've brought you three. The others are virtually repeats of these.' He put a photo down in front of Jackson. 'This is the last.'

'There was the tail end of a pickup going out of shot, the sidewalk, a fire hydrant and a background filled with one of the large residential buildings that framed that part of St Lawrence Street.'

'There's nobody in the shot Bob.'

'Nope. It was taken probably about four seconds after the first one: this one.' He put another picture down on the desk.

'What the …?' It was the same scene, minus the pickup. Instead the photo showed half a man. Probably less. He was completely missing from the top of his chest down. Half of the rest of him was missing. In fact all the shot showed was one shoulder and half a head. Jackson's brain was doing overtime.

Bob put the final photo on the desk. The middle one of the three.

'That's identical to the first one you showed me.'

'Not quite. Take another look.'

'The truck isn't in the shot.'

'Yup. But take another look.'

Jackson did. Knew he was missing something, but didn't know what. Then it hit him. 'There's a shadow of the man on the sidewalk and halfway up the wall behind him.'

'And no man in the photo.'

Chapter 3

HE knocked on the door.

'Come in.'

'Sir, sorry to trouble you, but there's someone acting suspiciously at the back of the shop.'

'In what way Brad?'

'He's been in there ages. Keeps taking stuff off the shelves, putting it back, moving things around.'

'You talked to him?'

'No sir, but …'

'What?'

'Well, it's kinda scary and he keeps taking bites outta some stuff, spitting it out and putting it back on the shelf.'

'Let's check it out.' Store manager Mike Staunton went next door, sat at the desk and surveyed the small bank of screens.

'There, sir.' Brad jabbed at one of the monitors. They watched, fascinated, as the man roamed around the back of the store, tasting things. Putting some back on the shelves and others in his pockets.

'Want me to ring the cops boss?'

'No, I think we can handle one guy don't you?'

'Go get Stevie and meet me down by the bakery.' When they were all together Mike led them down to the back where they'd last seen the man. They eventually found him fumbling around the cold unit. Cartons of milk, pots of cream and yoghurts lay scattered on the floor. The man had his back to them. Mike suddenly wondered about the wisdom of tackling this himself. He was a big guy; well over six-foot, wide shouldered and clearly muscular.

'Hey you! Stop what you're doing right now.'

He turned round. Mike gasped involuntarily and stopped dead in his tracks.

'Shit!' was all Brad could manage.

The man watched all three of them. Not warily, almost as if he was just studying them. Dressed in jeans and a sleeveless leather top, his arms were huge, neck thick and he had a large domed head with black hair plaited down his back. But it was not his powerful bulk that alarmed them. It was his eyes. They were a golden yellow colour. His stare seemed to penetrate to the very core of their beings.

'Cops boss,' whispered Brad.

'Think so. Stevie you stay here, Brad go make the call.'

The man spoke to them. Quiet and controlled. But it was a foreign language.

'You speak English?'

'Looks sort of Mexican boss,' said Stevie.

'Brad, just go.'

He only took one step. The thief's movement was nothing but a blur. Before anyone had grasped what was happening he had covered the several feet between them in a split second, grabbed Brad in one hand, lifted him off his feet and flung him into the shelves. Then he turned and looked at Mike. His legs turned to jelly under that yellow gaze.

'You best stop now before you get into any more trouble,' he said weakly. The thief grabbed him by the throat and said something. The pressure was light but Mike felt like the very life was being sucked out from inside him.

By this time there was a commotion behind the group. Two cops arrived and came up the aisle. The supermarket boss was dropped on the floor like a rag doll, unconscious. In one move the man was on the cops, grabbing them both at the same time and hurling them aside. In the blink of an eye he was out of the store.

Crolin stopped briefly on the sidewalk. Adjusted his eyes to the bright light. Behind him people were shouting. In the distance: a siren. He needed to get away. This had been a mistake. A big mistake because he'd put down a marker. The hunter wouldn't miss that.

It was just after 2 pm when Art Williams rang Jackson. 'We have something for you.'

'Ok Art, we'll be down there in about thirty minutes.'

'I need to warn you in advance that this isn't going to be straightforward.' The silence was heavy. 'You there, Jackson?'

'Yes.' It was a guarded response.

'What's the matter?'

'Not sure I'm ready for another surprise.'

'Another?'

'Can't explain right now Art. I hope it ain't going

to freak me out.' He put down the phone.

'Second surprise chief? What was the first?'

'Not your concern just now McClure. We'll have a briefing before you hit the St Lawrence Street quarter tonight.'

McClure wondered about warning Lisa he might be late, but felt sure he could wrap all that up before their dinner date. The photos of the victim had already been sent to the Maine divisions. They'd wait for a response before moving it further afield. In the meantime McClure had tracked down the store where the victim's coat had come from.

'You want me to check this out chief?' he said waving his sheet of paper at Jackson.

'Leave it 'til after we've been down to the path lab. We'll take it from there. Art seems to think he has something interesting on his hands so might be useful if you cut in as well.'

Jackson swung the car into Maine Medical Centre's car park just off Bramhall Street, locked up and headed into reception. They took the lift down to the path lab and asked for Art Williams.

'Take a seat Officer, he'll be here shortly.'

It was quiet. Jackson and McClure were the only ones apparently waiting for anything. A couple of white coats with clipboards drifted past chatting. There were a few nurses going about their business and the woman on reception was battering away at the computer keyboard, interrupted once by a phone call. Art finally appeared after about 15 minutes, kicking his way through some swing doors to their right.

'Sorry to keep you waiting Jackson.' He shook hands with both the officers. They followed him back through the doors, down a corridor, turned right through some more swing doors and into an office.

'So, what's not straightforward about this?' asked Jackson.

'Bang to the point as usual eh? Well, I could sit down and explain it to you, but it might be best if you come through.'

The post-mortem room was functional. The ceiling a mass of covered strip lights, the walls white, down one side was a long metal bench with a sink at one end and a couple of wall-mounted microscopes.

In the centre were two metal slabs mounted on cylinders and on the other side a couple of trolleys and a rack of instruments. One slab was empty. On the other lay the victim, covered with a sheet. It was Art's place of work and not one that either Jackson or McClure cared for.

'You can leave us for now Jessica.' Art's assistant went out. 'It's difficult to know where to start.'

'Maybe tell us how he died?' said McClure.

'Oh that can certainly wait.'

Jackson raised an eyebrow.

'I'm not sure how well up you two are on human anatomy, but we have here a couple of — how shall I say — oddities. So we'll go straight to the big factor first.' He drew back the cloth. Looked at both men. 'I hope you're not going to pass out on me.' The victim's chest was still opened up. McClure swallowed, Jackson was unmoved. He'd seen worse. The pathologist produced a small metal rod and pointed into the chest. 'Know what that is?'

'The heart,' said Jackson.

He used the rod to push the organ slightly to

one side and pointed underneath it. 'And that?'

Jackson looked at Art. 'Well, under normal circumstances, I'd say another heart.'

'And you'd be correct.' He pulled up the sheet and led them back into his office. 'Evolution, genetics. It's all a very funny business. As a species we follow a basic conformity but every now and then the whole process throws up what we call a mutation or an abnormality. I'm sure you don't need me to tell you the sorts of things we're talking about. However, a human having two hearts isn't one of them.'

'Until now,' ventured Jackson.

'Well, I'm afraid the jury's out on that one Jackson.'

'There's more?'

'In good time. The only humans to have a double heart are a rare few who, in the process of a heart transplant, have also kept their original heart. I won't bore you with the medical reasons behind that.'

'So where does that leave us?'

'What do you know about the octopus?'

'Less than I do about human biology.'

'Well, they have three hearts. Two branchial hearts that pump blood through each of the two gills while the third pumps blood through the body. But it's the reason for multi-hearts rather than the number.'

'Please keep it simple,' said Jackson.

'Because of the conditions in which they live their body needs to be able to pump blood around in either normal circumstances or in cold conditions when oxygen pressure changes dramatically. In other words they have two systems for oxygen transportation depending on the temperature their bodies are facing.'

'Are you saying the victim lived under water?' asked McClure.

Art laughed. 'Good gracious me, no! He has no gills for a kick off. He would drown as easily as you McClure.'

Jackson said nothing.

'What I'm saying is that the evolutionary process in the victim has equipped him to live at different temperatures. And those temperature extremes are obviously considerably different to those we face on earth, otherwise we'd all have two hearts.' He smiled at both officers; pleased with his logical reasoning. They sat dumfounded.

'Are you saying he's an alien?' Jackson almost whispered.

'I'm not saying anything Jackson. I'm just explaining the laws of physiology to you and how they relate to the development of the human body as we understand it. And where the victim sits in relation to all that.'

Jackson shook his head, as if trying to dislodge colliding thoughts in his brain. He rubbed his temples hard with his hand. First the photos and now this. Still not half a day old and already this murder investigation seemed to be spiralling out of anything like normal.

'Boss?'

'Yes, McClure?'

'I'm not sure I understand all this, but ...'

'I haven't finished yet,' interrupted the pathologist. 'Naturally your guys came to take finger prints. They couldn't get any.' He shifted in his chair. 'Now before you start, this is not completely unusual. There is a condition called *adermatoglyphia* which leaves people without any finger prints. But it is very rare.'

'So?'

'So, given what we've already come across, I want to carry out further tests on the victim's skin before reaching any conclusions.'

'It still doesn't answer the double heart though,' said McClure.

'Indeed.'

Jackson's brain was racing. A man who only half-appeared in a photograph before disappearing in the next shot a split second later and a victim with two hearts which were needed for living in the sorts of conditions you don't find on Earth. He felt the first twinge of a headache. And that niggling again deep in his stomach.

Chapter 4

MCCLURE'S questioning of other people in the neighbourhood had been virtually futile. People 'hadn't heard anything'. It didn't help his mood with the rain coming on and the night cold, but not cold enough to turn it to snow just yet. That would come soon enough, thought McClure. He had got impatient with at least two people in the block where Beth Donald lived.

'If she can hear that racket last night how come you can't?' he'd snapped at one woman. He knew she was lying, but what could he do? Her husband had yanked the front door wider — McClure hadn't been invited in — and left him in no mind as to what he thought about the cop calling his wife a liar in all but name. The only help, if you could call it that, came from someone who lived up on the second floor of the block by the alley. He thought he might have heard something. Questioned further, he shrugged his shoulders.

By the time McClure arrived down on the

harbour front to meet up with Lisa he was in a foul mood — and late. The sidewalk glistened in the rain and out in the harbour waves slapped the boats. He walked past a couple of chowder huts, their windows steamed up. Laughter and chatter burst into the night as a door opened. McClure dodged the traffic as he crossed the street and headed down to the newly developed end of the front. A couple of hotels, shops, cafe bars and restaurants had brought a new style of life to the area. Not everyone in Portland liked it. Many still preferred the old docks with the piers, lobster boats and chowder houses. But large warehouses that had fallen into disuse had been knocked down for the development so now the new was rubbing shoulders with the old. McClure was of the younger generation. And they approved.

The old-fashioned style, dark wood frames and huge bow windows of *Caltronio's* gave a panoramic view of the harbour front. McClure went in, glanced at his watch: fifteen minutes late. He hoped Lisa wasn't mad. He was led to a table just inside the window. She was sitting there, a bottle of red wine already served, a glass half empty in front of her.

He bent down and pecked her on the offered cheek. 'Really sorry I'm late Lisa. Just making some calls in St Lawrence Street. God some of those people are a pain in the ass.'

'It's ok Sam. I've been enjoying the view and the wine.' She picked up her glass and tilted it towards him. 'So how's the investigation going?'

'Ok.'

She caught his reticence. 'Not want to talk about it then?'

Since the visit to the path lab, Jackson and McClure hadn't really been sure where to go with everything. And once Jackson had filled his sergeant in on the photos they still couldn't get to grips with what they had. Didn't know where to take the case. It was McClure who came out with the back to basics line; *Just make our enquiries as normal chief and see where they lead.*

Jackson had nodded. It made sense for now. McClure shook his head when Lisa asked the question. 'It's not that I don't want to. I can't. There's stuff we can't let anywhere near the public arena just now.'

Lisa huffed. 'You don't trust me then.'

She'd set a trap, but McClure wasn't about to walk into it. 'So how's life among the rocks and fossils?'

'It's been really interesting. We've had some new stuff come in from Peru for an exhibition after Christmas. We're sorting through it all at the moment.' She went on to tell him about artefacts, ancient tribes and strange customs. It was fascinating, but he was partly preoccupied.

It was when they were halfway through their main course that McClure saw Mr Pilkington. He was walking past the window. McClure leaped out of his chair, knocking over his wine glass and scattering cutlery across the floor.

'Sam!'

He shot out of *Caltronio's* and saw the man loping down the street. He was positive it was the same one Jackson had pointed out standing on the sidewalk when they left the murder scene that morning; the half-a-man in the photos Jackson had shown him that afternoon. McClure kept at a safe distance and watched as he entered the Harbor

View hotel a few minutes later. He waited briefly outside and saw the man hand a key in at reception. He headed back to the restaurant.

Inside they were still cleaning up the mess and had moved Lisa to another table. McClure offered his abject apologies to the waiters. Lisa looked at him, a warning flare glinting in her eyes. He held up his hands in mock surrender.

'Look I'm really, really sorry Lisa. It was urgent.'

She nodded. A motion that suggested he should continue without comment from her.

'I think I saw someone we're looking for. I just needed to see where he was headed. Sounds a bit lame. I'm truly sorry.'

'Remember when we broke up last year Sam? I told you that your job was getting in the way of our time too much?' She tilted her head towards the door. 'Sort of like that.'

It wasn't the only reason, but he wasn't about to open that can of worms just now. He still needed her help to start with. 'What can I say? If the guy hadn't walked past the window everything would have been a little more comfortable.' He shrugged.

'Just reminds me of why we split. Which I guess might be useful in case you suggest anything about us hooking up again.' Then she smiled. 'You better get us another bottle of wine.'

'I've got a better idea. Let's go to *The Lobster* bar for a nightcap.'

He paid the bill and they headed out into the wet night.

The Lobster was a popular bar in the Harbor View Hotel. As the rain turned to a heavy downpour they dashed the last few yards and burst into reception. McClure had a quick look in case his man was around. There was no sign. Not unexpected. They sat in a quiet corner on a deep sofa. A waiter took their drinks order. A Jack Daniels and coke for McClure and Pernod and coke for Lisa.

'So this man …?'

'It's someone Jackson saw at the crime scene today. He was taking a very close interest in what we were doing. We got the forensics boys to get a shot of him. He was on the sidewalk across the road. So we're trying to ID him.'

'Obvious question, but I'm not the detective; why didn't you stop and question him then?'

'Not sure to be honest. It was Jackson's call and he didn't make it. He had his reasons, but not sure I'd have passed up the opportunity. Still I just needed to see where he went.'

'And where did he go.'

'In here.'

'Oh right. So you take a girl out for dinner and then tag her along afterwards while you're working!'

The edge in her voice made McClure cautious. 'Well, I was going to suggest we came here afterwards anyway. It's a cool bar and not far to go.' He waited. 'Anyway, like you said, it's not like we're trying to get anything back on track.'

That flustered her. She looked down and brushed an imaginary crease out of her skirt.

'Well, yes, that's true.'

There was a hint of a blush. And McClure didn't miss that. 'Of course, we could have dinner next week. As we're sort of good friends.'

She accepted, rather too quickly thought McClure. He realised he still had a soft spot for the girl from the museum.

'Look do you mind if I just check with reception?'

'You want to book a room for us tonight?' She looked at him with mocking wide-eyes. Then laughed, lightly touched his arm and nodded towards the desk. 'Go on Sam.'

Ryan watched the man walk over. He'd seen the young couple walk in. 'They'll want a room,' he said quietly to himself.

'Hello. I'm trying to check if you have a particular guy staying at this hotel.'

'We have several sir,' said Ryan in his best officious, clipped voice.

'He's just over six foot, longish black hair, quite skinny and about 190 pounds. He came in about twenty minutes ago. He was wearing a long dark coat. No hat.'

'I'm sure you appreciate, sir,' he emphasised the *sir*, 'that our guests can stay at this hotel in the knowledge that this is a confidential arrangement between themselves and the hotel.' He gave a thin smile after what he thought was his trump card.

It wasn't, of course. McClure pulled his police ID and held it discreetly in front of Ryan.

He looked at it and looked back to McClure. 'Well, why didn't you say?'

'The guest ...' He made a point of staring at Ryan's badge; '... Mr Ingalls?'

'I really need to talk to the office manager.'

'No, you don't. All you need to do is give me his name and room number.'

Secretly Ryan was, of course, intrigued. He made of point of checking the register. 'He is in room 512, fifth floor. The name is Mr Gary Pilkington.' He shut the book. 'I do hope this isn't going to be a public business ... in the hotel. We do have a reputation to maintain.'

'Nothing for you to worry about just now Mr Ingalls. We're only making inquiries.' He put a card on the desk. 'I'd be grateful if you learn any information about Mr Pilkington, if you were to give me a call.' He winked and walked back to Lisa.

Ryan looked at the card. *Well, well. A bit of excitement!*

Ocean Avenue was a misleading name. It wasn't really near the ocean at all. The road mimicked the curve of Back Cove, the large inlet cutting in from the sea around the point on which downtown Portland sat. Between the avenue and the cove sat a small, lace network of residential roads. It was actually Baxter Boulevard which followed the cove's water edge running past the housing development, sports ground and Payson Park before plugging back into *Route 295*. Crolin was walking down George Street between Ocean Avenue and Baxter Boulevard. It was dark, cold and raining. The big man wasn't frightened, but wary — always wary — and now concerned.

Once near the house, he cut through some shrubs and trees and made his way up to the back door. He pushed it open, listened intently. Then went inside. His eyes quickly adjusted. Once through to the front room, he checked the street to make sure nobody had followed. He'd be surprised if anyone was on his trail just yet. Then he went upstairs, lay down on the bed and thought.

It had been a bad day. The death was

unfortunate, the store episode stupid but, most important of all, he had now lost the second part of the key. Not only did it underline the fact that he was trapped, for he'd found himself in that place when losing the first part, but it meant that if the hunter got his hands on both parts of the key, Crolin was in serious trouble. His options had become severely limited. If the hunter tracked him down, either Crolin would be neutralised and taken back, or Crolin would kill the hunter and never get back. Ever. Unless he could lay his hands on the two keys to the Gatetrap.

Jackson was back in his office by seven the next morning. He'd slept little as his brain turned over yesterday's events again and again. McClure had been right of course; he had to set on one side the two extraordinary events that had unfolded and tackle the investigation in his normal methodical manner. But he couldn't stop himself slipping back to the photos and the news from the post-mortem. However his first course was to try and identify the two men: the victim and the man on the sidewalk. So he set about making out his list: the actions and the questions. McClure arrived an hour later armed with two cups of coffee.

'A welcome sight and smell.' said Jackson.

McClure put the cups down on the desk and fished a piece of paper out of his pocket. He put it in front of Jackson. The detective read it, without touching it and then looked up at his sergeant.

'So who is Mr Gary Pilkington?'

'The man on the sidewalk.'

Jackson leant back in his chair, impressed but not showing it. 'For sure?'

'For sure chief. I saw him last night down the harbour front while having dinner.'

Jackson raised his eyebrows.

'Expensive place for a sergeant of Portland Police department to be eating.'

'I was with Lisa.'

'Ah, impressing her uh?'

McClure ignored the jibe and went on to explain what had happened.

'We got a tail on him yet?'

'I called Doug last night. I told him it was strictly

between the three of us for now so he staked it out last night. He's still there.'

Jackson glanced at his watch. 'We owe him one. Big time. Let's go.' Jackson strode out of the office. McClure raced after him carrying two coffees.

'Oh. And good work McClure,' he shouted over his shoulder.

Jackson tapped on the car window. Detective Doug Blain rolled it down.

'Hiya, chief. He ain't left the building yet.'

'Thanks Doug. Go get some sleep, but come back in at four I need you in on this and will brief you then. Meantime, say nothing.'

Blain pulled out into the traffic and McClure reversed their car into the space opposite the Harbor View Hotel. They drank their coffees whilst going over what they had so far.

'Right. We need to trace Mr Pilkington.' said Jackson.

The sergeant reached for his laptop on the seat behind them and fired it up. Then he went into the usual search routine. Local police files, city residential files, driving licence files … the screen flickered through it all. And revealed no Mr Gary Pilkington looking remotely like their target. 'Could be an alias.'

'Indeed,' said Jackson, 'but it's all we got and it's where we start. Put a general in and see if he shows up on any other neighbouring states data banks.'

Mr Pilkington emerged from the hotel just after ten. He was dressed in the same floor-length dark raincoat. He stood for a few minutes looking up and down Thames Street then set off along the harbour front towards Commercial Street.

'Right tail him this side,' said Jackson. 'I'll cross over and follow on the other side. We'll alternate the close tail as usual so we lessen the chances of alarming him.'

Mr Pilkington's long loping stride ate up the ground fast. He went past Maine State Pier and then cut right up Pearl Street. Jackson fell behind, losing time crossing the busy Commercial Street so McClure closed up. It was halfway up Pearl Street that Mr Pilkington completely disappeared. One minute he was there, just a few yards in front of the sergeant, the next minute he was gone.

'He must have turned off,' said Jackson when he finally caught up.

'Where?' said McClure. 'There's no doors here. Just brick walls and windows. Any doors are either behind us or further up there.' He waved up the street.

'Well, he can't have vanished into thin air, damn it. You sure you were paying attention properly son?' McClure felt his face colour up at the unfair accusation and was about to cut loose when Jackson gripped his arm. 'There!' He pointed up the street and there was Mr Pilkington walking towards Newbury Street junction.

McClure shook his head. 'I don't get it chief. I tell you he vanished.'

'Forget it, let me do the close tail from here.' Jackson walked off and McClure crossed to the other sidewalk. Then he saw Jackson stop, look around, walk a couple of paces, stop again and scratch his head. McClure crossed over. 'Chief?'

'He's vanished.'

McClure opened his mouth, then thought better of a smart retort. This time Mr Pilkington did not reappear.

As daylight seeped through the curtains, Crolin was trying to draw up a plan of action. He really needed to get back to the alley and find the second part of the key. Yesterday the place had been swarming with people. Today, hopefully, it might be quieter. He slipped on the sleeveless leather jerkin, his sunglasses and checked in the top pocket. Just to make sure the device was still there. After snacking quickly on some of the stuff he had stolen from the store yesterday, he headed out the back door, cut through the shrubs and back on to George Street. As he walked briskly round the corner into Ocean Avenue he bumped into a cop.

'Easy man,' The cop bristled and gently pushed Crolin away. His problem was that people just didn't walk anywhere around here. They all got about in vehicles. 'You live round here?' he asked, taking in the rough clothing.

Crolin didn't answer.

'You live round here?' This time the friendly edge had dropped out of the question.

Crolin was angry with himself for getting caught out like this. Yet another mistake. He was making too many now. The officer reached into his top pocket to pull out his notebook. It was not a good move.

'So what the hell was that all about?' asked Jackson.

'It was just like I said chief, right?'

'Yeh.' Jackson rubbed the space just above his nose. It was an unconscious action. He did it when he was perplexed. 'You know, I'm beginning to wonder if I'm going nuts. How can a guy disappear like that? Not just once, but twice. How can I see him one minute and not the next minute?'

'You're asking the wrong man chief.'

'The trouble is McClure, I don't know who is the right man to ask.'

They were walking back to the car. McClure went inside the hotel and approached reception.

''Scuse me.'

'Yes, sir?'

'Could you tell me when Mr Ingalls is back on reception?'

'May I ask who wants to know?' asked the woman behind the desk. McClure showed her his card. She nodded. 'He's back on duty at 5pm. Shall I tell him you called?'

The sergeant said not to bother, he'd call back later. He climbed back into the car. 'What now chief?'

'Back to the station. We need to carry out more checks, see if forensics have come up with anything I can deal with yet. I need to ring Art and see if he's got anything else on our man from outer space.' McClure roared. Jackson indicated, pulled out into the traffic and started heading back, driving up Pearl Street, past where Mr Pilkington had disappeared and turning into Middle Street.

Suddenly the radio burst into life. *Code red! Code red*!

McClure switched frequencies.

We gotta a cop down. Repeat a cop down. On the junction of Ocean Boulevard and George Street. Cop down on junction of Ocean Boulevard and

George Street. Available units report in.

'McClure and Jackson here. We're on our way. Repeat, on our way now.'
Jackson slapped the siren on the roof and floored the accelerator.

Lisa Schwark was confused. On two fronts. What mostly occupied her thoughts was last night. She had promised herself before meeting Sam to hold him at arm's length. There was no way back into that relationship for her, she'd decided. Too often his work got in the way for one thing, resulting in her being let down because he was still stuck on some case or other, or having to suddenly leave after getting a call. She found it disrupting and intrusive. They'd rowed about it a few times. Eventually they sat down, talked it out in a non-hostile manner and went their separate ways. They both regretted it.

But all her resolve quickly evaporated when they met up at Caltronio's. Despite the fact that he was late. Despite the fact he shot out in the middle of the meal attracting everyone's attention in the place. Despite the fact that he used the, *let's have a nightcap* line to get into the hotel where the man had gone. The thing is that Sam was very likeable and also courteous. Not many men were these days. She always felt safe and valued in his company. And he made her laugh a lot. She was cross with herself for blushing when he reminded her they were now *just good friends* and equally cross for too eagerly accepting another dinner date. Now though it all made her smile to herself. The thought of Sam gave her a warmth she'd missed.

Lisa was also confused about the photos scattered on the desk in front of her.

After leaving Portland High and then after completing her initial training she had joined the museum initially as a technician, largely just taking care of various items. While doing that she started specialising in ancient Native American Indian artefacts and soon became renowned for her expertise in symbols, charm stones and decorated pottery of that particular culture. Within the museum she moved on to become a conservator, preserving and treating artefacts and carrying out substantial historical, scientific and archaeological research.

Privately she was also fascinated by Greek mythology, had completed a home-based tuition course, reading about it avidly.

She'd realised before of course that, like Sam, she was also into detective work. So she did understand the driving motives behind his work. And the photos fascinated her. 'I'd really like to get my hands on that,' she murmured, tucking her hair behind one ear. She was still puzzled by the symbol on one side of the object. It resembled nothing in her line of work and she resolved to talk to a couple of other conservators who moved in different fields and might be able to give her a lead. There was what looked like a sphere on one side, but it had a jagged split running through it, some sort of scroll work carved underneath and hieroglyphs round the top. The reverse was completely smooth apart from a slight crater-style indentation bang in the middle.

It was only when she put the photo under a lighted magnifying screen that she realised the edge of the object was quite intricate. It was slightly thicker than a quarter, but the whole edge was a series of notches. For a minute it niggled at her, then she realised it was a bit like the edge of a key.

Mr Pilkington sat in a wing chair by the window in his room. He absently turned a small black box over and over in his hand while planning his next move. Evading the cops earlier had been a simple enough business, but he was beginning to think that somehow he was going to need their help. He certainly didn't want them getting to Crolin before he did. He looked at the device. If only he knew where the keys were, then this would soon be over.

There were already three patrol cars and an ambulance at the scene by the time Jackson and McClure arrived. An officer lifted the tape for them to pass under and they headed over to the sidewalk.

'What's happened?'

Brett Rotsko turned round. 'Hi, Jackson.' A cop down always brought out the big guns, but it must be three or four years since that had happened in Portland.

'Who is he Brett?'

'Officer Kistner. He's in a bad way. The medics

are doing some emergency stuff on him now and then will whip him off to hospital.'

Jackson looked round. Apart from the police, there were only five other people gathered at the scene outside the tapes. A couple of officers were talking to them, notebooks in hand. Folk from a residential area like this were mostly out at work.

'Where's his partner and who is it?'

'Loey. She was in the car which they'd parked up on the corner of Austin Street and Kistner was just taking a stroll down here. Nothing special apparently, just a call in on the neighbourhood.'

'We got an APB out?'

'We only just got here Jackson. All we've done is throw up a ring round Bay Cove.'

'Is he going to be ok chief?' McClure nodded towards the ambulance into which the cop was now being loaded.

'We're not sure. Apart from a nasty bang on the head, he doesn't appear to have any other injuries. But the medics are worried about his condition. Signals ain't good.'

'Mind if I talk to Loey?' asked Jackson.

'No problems. It'll probably land on your desk anyway.'

Jackson huffed. 'I'm pretty busy just now Brett.' He walked across to the officer.

'How you doing, Loey?'

'I'm ok Sir, just worried about Jack.'

'Of course. So what you got here?'

Loey was sitting on a low wall, legs stretched out in front. She looked down the street as if trying to recapture the scene. 'Jack said to park up here and that he was going to take a short stroll down Ocean Avenue, make sure all the locals were behaving themselves. He got to the corner of George Street and this big guy came out the shrubs at him.'

'What do you mean … *came out the shrubs?* Like he jumped him?'

'Not exactly, Sir. It was like he was taking a short-cut and collided with Jack. He put his hand out to try and stop the collision. The big guy sorta grabbed Jack by the throat and he just dropped to the sidewalk. Like he'd been knocked unconscious. It was really strange Sir.'

McClure had been silent. There was a little

alarm going off deep inside him. 'What do you mean by a big guy?'

'Well, big Sir, large.'

'You're a cop. Be a little more specific, just like they trained you.'

The rebuke brought her back in line. 'Sorry, Sir. He was well over six foot, at least 240 lbs, but not fat if you know what I mean Sir.'

'Sure,' said McClure; 'Just well built and I'm guessing shoulders probably bigger than normal. Someone who'd make a quarter back look skinny?'

'Yes Sir.'

'It's our man chief.' They walked away from the officer. 'But what in the hell is he doing out here?'

'You want my guess? He's holed up round here somewhere. I think we need to start asking some questions and start poking around.'

Jackson nodded again, 'Let's go back and get a team on it.'

They gave the description to Brett who ordered an APB. As they were driving back McClure talked about a breakthrough, but Jackson still wasn't happy.

'We still haven't a name for the victim, we don't

have a motive and we still have a coupla of very strange issues to get our heads round. Otherwise it's going great.'

Although the rain had cleared up from the previous night, the sky was still overcast. That morning forecasters had warned locals to expect the first snow of the season; about two to four inches carried in by a nor'easter that had blown up overnight. Already the first few flakes were beginning to fall. Crolin had seen it before, though the cold wasn't particularly a problem for him. However he realised he was beginning to look out of place in his sleeveless leather jerkin and sunglasses. The jerkin he could do something about, the glasses he couldn't. He knew his eyes were an unusual colour here — which he found strange — and would mark him out.

Crolin stopped not far from the alley, leant against a wall and looked round. He wondered if the hunter would be staking out the kill spot. It was a gamble coming back, but he had to find the other part of the key. Crolin finally ducked into the alley and merged in with the shadows down one side. He began searching. He found nothing on the ground and climbed steadily up the fire escape reaching the window he'd tried to get through. Again, nothing. For the first time Crolin felt a brief stab of fear. He would now have to hunt the hunter. And you just didn't do that. Nobody ever won that game.

Chapter 5

THE APB failed. Most of them do. As Jackson had expected, the attacker — their suspect — had slipped through the net. The patrol cars were sent back to normal duty and the incident was added to the slowly growing pile of information. But not a lot of it was joining up just now. Jackson was still aware he hadn't properly filled Rotsko in on the developments. He picked up the phone. 'Brett, you got ten? Good I'll be right up. Oh – and you're going to need a strong coffee for this one.'

He pushed open the door. Rotsko was seated at the long table in his office with two mugs. Jackson sat down.

'So what you got for me?' He noticed the quick frown.

'Let me give you the short version. We have a murder victim in the alley. We have a witness who saw the victim and another man go into the alley. We gotta a pretty good idea that the guy who took down Kistner is the same one and we traced the guy who was watching us too closely when we were at the alley.'

'Sounds promising.'

'He's staying at the Harbor View.'

'You questioned him yet?'

'Nope. Didn't want to spook him too early so me and McClure tailed him this morning.'

'So what's the bad news?' Rotsko had sensed there was something to come almost from the outset and that Jackson would hold it back.

'Well, it's not exactly bad, more weird in a kind of *oh shit* fashion!' He then filled his chief in on the photos, the post-mortem and the disappearing Mr Pilkington. 'Thing is I can string an investigation together as well as anybody. Plan it out, chase down the details, prioritise the line of info we need, fan out the investigation at the right point. But this stuff ...' He tailed off. Left it in the air.

Rotsko said nothing. He got up, went over to the window and looked down on the city.

'To be honest Jackson, I don't know what to say to you. There has to be an explanation, just has to be. Logically it adds up somewhere, but just now I can't see where.' The phone on his desk rang. 'Hello. Yup he's here.' He held it out. It was Art. He was ready for Jackson to return to the path lab. 'Mind if I tag along?' asked Rotsko already slipping on his jacket and not waiting for an answer.

Jackson, Rotsko and McClure were sitting in Art's office. It wasn't big so it was a little crowded.

Eventually the pathologist arrived. 'Hi people. My we have a growing audience. How you doing Brett?'

'Good thanks Art. But let's cut to the issue. You've given Jackson something of a headache my friend.'

Art laughed. 'Well, I'm afraid it's going to get worse. You better come with me.'

Instead of taking them down to the post-mortem room, he led them along to a large office. It had no external windows, just a bank of glass down one wall overlooking a wide internal corridor. Art drew the blinds across them. At one end of the table a screen was lowered from the ceiling.

'Right, I'm afraid it's going to be another

biology lesson.'

Jackson groaned.

'What now Art?' asked McClure. 'The guy got three brains?' It didn't provoke a laugh.

'A little bit more subtle than that Sergeant.' He switched on the laptop, hit a few buttons and a diagram appeared on the screen. 'Now gentleman, that cube is a cross section of the human skin. Here's a few basic facts. I'll try and keep it simple again. Our skin is made up of multiple layers of tissue. Its job is to guard our muscles, bones, ligaments and internal organs.'

'Like a parcel I guess,' ventured McClure.

Art ignored him. 'The skin interfaces with the environment and plays a key role in protecting the body against pathogens and excessive water loss. You've heard of pigmentation?'

They all nodded.

'Good. There are five different pigmentations which determine our skin colour and these pigments occur at different levels and different places in the skin.' He moved his cursor to point them out on the diagram. 'One pigment, melanin, is brown in colour and keratin covers yellow to orange.' He looked at each of them in turn, making sure no eyes had glazed over. 'You still with this?'

'Yup,' said Jackson.

'Right. Now we get to the interesting bit.' He brought another graphic up on the screen. A close up of part of the skin section. 'Humans have three primary skin layers. They are the epidermis, dermis and hypodermis; here, here and here. I won't tax your brains with their functions. So, on to our John.' He paused, took a drink of water.

'You already know about the fingerprints. We cannot account in any way at all for the absence of those. What I can tell you though is that he has a fourth primary skin layer.' He looked at the three men, their faces blank. As he expected it had no impact. The enormity of this biological fact would pass them by.

'What does that mean?' asked Jackson.

'I'll answer that by telling you that this is never found in a human being. Ever. We have evolved with three primary skin layers because that is all we need for our skins to function wherever we live in the world.'

'Right,' said Rotsko.

'It doesn't stop there either. In this fourth layer we found pigments. These were pigments which are not found in humans either. They control a range of colours: red, blue, yellow and white.'

'You're losing me now,' said Jackson.

'Well, put simply, just as human pigments give us the range of skin colours you see, so these pigments also give a range of colours depending on how they mix.'

'You mean people with these pigments might not only be brown, black or white, but could be red, blue, purple or any combination?' The question came from McClure.

'Quite.'

'You telling me this guy's a freakin' alien?'

'No McClure. I'm telling you no such thing. My job is just to let you know what we found. You're the detective.' He smiled thinly.

'What else?' asked Jackson.

'There is something called chromatophores. What these do is rapidly relocate particles of pigment thereby influencing the skin colour. These chromatophores change because the cells get a message from the brain and change the colour.'

'Go on,' said Jackson.

'It's a function of the skin that is found in the chameleon.'

'Oh shit,' said McClure. 'Pearl Street and the photos of Mr Pilkington.'

Crolin stood still. He quickly blended into the background by the shrubs and watched as the two cops walked past. He was in something of a dilemma, knowing that his hideaway had been compromised. But he needed to retrieve the bag. As soon as they disappeared round the corner, he moved quickly to the back of the house and in through the door. He waited, listening. A car drove past, but that was the only sound.

Crolin went up stairs, picked the small leather bag off the floor and emptied the contents onto the bed. He lifted the lid on a small, platinum-coloured box. Inside were two empty compartments; one the shape of a disc, the other a triangle-shaped hole.

They were designed to hold things snugly. He muttered and closed the lid. He opened another large box. Inside was a rectangular black device with two small buttons on the top. He pulled it out, pushed one and a green LED glowed softly. Then the unit started humming. He switched it off and pushed the other button. A yellow LED began winking. It was as far as he could go. He switched that off and closed the lid and put it all back in the bag.

Just then he heard someone trying the front door handle. Crolin froze. He could hear talking outside. The door rattled hard. Then silence.

'In here.' The voice was at the back and then he heard the two cops moving about downstairs.

'How long's this place been empty?'

'The guy down the street said 'bout three months.'

'Well, it's been used since then. Take a look at this.'

The cops had moved into the kitchen. Had found the bits of food he'd been using.

'This looks like his base. Shall we call in?'

'Let's check the rest of the place first.'

Crolin could hear them moving about downstairs. Then the stairs creaked. The cops were talking as they moved away from his room down the landing. He heard doors opening and closing. Then they came towards his room. The door opened. Crolin stood stock still. Faded into the dark background.

'Someone's been sleeping here for sure.'

'Look at this.' One had picked Crolin's bag off the bed and was rifling through it. He handed one of the boxes to his colleague who opened it. It was the empty one.

'What the hell's that for?'

'Beats me. Look at this one.' He pressed one of the buttons and the green light glowed gently, before finally fading out.

'Right let's get this back to the car and call in.' As the officers passed him Crolin grabbed one round the neck, pulling him tight to his body as the man gave a gargling cry.

'What the …?' The second officer pulled out his gun and levelled it at the pair of them.

'Let him go. Now!'

Crolin stood there. The cop shouted at him again, raised his gun up and fired it at the ceiling, then aimed back at Crolin and the other cop. The sound of the shot boomed through the room fading away to silence. Gun outstretched the cop slowly approached. Crolin moved lightning fast, dropping the semi-conscious officer to the ground. He grabbed the gun, viciously bending the cop's arm back. There was a crack as the arm snapped and the cop screamed out. Crolin flung him across the room. Then something hit him hard across the back of the head and darkness swarmed in.

The silence in the room began to weigh heavily. Rotsko, Jackson and McClure didn't know what to say. Art had said all he had to say. The three cops were staring at the screen seeing nothing. Their minds were in overdrive.

'Perhaps I can help you with a recap,' said Art. 'Just to help you get focussed.'

'I don't know if it's going to be any help at all,' said Jackson.

'Nonetheless. The victim has two hearts. Both are natural and clearly operate depending on the extremes of oxygen pressure he faces. Secondly he has no fingerprints; again this seems entirely natural for this person. Finally he has the skin system I explained to you. In principle it would seem to operate in the same way as a chameleon: a form of camouflage. Of course we would need to see that in action to confirm it as a fact.'

'We may be able to help you there, Art.' Jackson explained about the photographs.

'There is another question which you haven't answered yet, Art.'

'What's that?'

'How did he die?'

'Well, that's very difficult. There is no obvious cause of death other than at some point the victim stopped breathing. There's little damage to the body other than some cuts and bruising, none of which were obviously fatal.'

'Can you tell us anything about those?' asked Jackson.

'I would say they are the result of a fight or a

scuffle, but as I said nothing serious or fatal. Mostly they're to the head and arms and some heavy bruising on one shoulder. Probably where he hit the ground.'

'Because of the hearts and the more complex muscle and blood vessel systems around them I cannot even determine whether or not he had a heart attack. If he was a normal human you'd say he died of natural causes.'

'But you're not going to say that for this guy, are you?' ventured Rotsko.

'To be honest Brett there is nothing I can say. I will write up my report of course and at some point after the investigation, because of his physiology, a lot of important people in the medical world are going to want an 'in' on this.'

'But not until I say so,' growled Jackson.

'Of course. We will keep him here and wait for you to complete the case.'

'Damned if I know how the hell we're going to do that with all this.' Jackson stood up. 'Well, I guess we ought to thank you Art, but it's causing a lot of confusion.'

'You've not said, Art, what your opinion is of all this,' said Rotsko.

Art smiled. 'I'm bloody fascinated of course. I wouldn't say he's an alien. He's not green and got one eye. But he's not strictly a human being either. What you must realise gentlemen is that you have something much, much bigger than a murder investigation on your hands.'

The first thing he heard was the screaming. Then he was aware of someone sitting on his back tying his wrists together with something.

The cop on his back was talking to the other. 'It's ok buddy, it's ok. I've got him restrained, we'll get help now. You'll soon be fixed.'

The other one's screams kept fading to a whimper. He finally sunk into a low moan, punctuated with 'Oh my god.'

Crolin lifted his head a fraction. The cop slammed it back to the ground. 'You stay right there, pal. We got you.' Crolin understood nothing but the anger in the voice. He felt something yanked hard round his wrists. But he felt no pain. He flexed against what was tying his wrists together. Knew it wasn't going to be a problem, but he would prefer to be on his feet. The cop stood up, put one foot on his back and reached for his radio. He started the call. Then, again, all hell broke loose.

Crolin tensed his shoulders and upper arms then, with an explosion of energy, shattered the cuffs which clattered to the floor. He rolled sideways, grabbed the cop's foot and twisted it hard. As he crashed to the floor, Crolin was up on his feet. The radio had spun away from the cop. There were urgent voices coming out of it. Crolin stamped on it. Hard. He turned to find the man reaching again for his gun. Crolin kicked it out of his hand, reached down, grabbed him by his throat and lifted him to his feet. Fear was pouring out of his eyes; his partner was moaning and shouting in the corner. The cop felt only light pressure on the throat. But no pain. He was staring into the yellow eyes. They were flat, showed nothing. And he just felt the life ebbing out of him.

She was working on her speech. Trish Longton

was due to address the Portland Chamber at their monthly meeting in a couple of days and would be dealing with the funding issues that the Medical Centre faced. The scientists at the Centre's Research Institute were carrying out some ground-breaking work into the use of hormone treatments that could help in the fight against diabetes. Money was always a problem and here was a chance to raise the profile among the city's business community. The phone rang.

'Hello. Oh hello, Jackson.'

'Trish I've got a problem and I really need your brains on this one. Though I'm not sure you'll be much help.'

'I wouldn't rule me out that quickly, Jackson. What's the problem?'

'It's difficult to explain. We've had a couple of meetings with Art Williams following a PM on that victim off St Lawrence Street and it's thrown up some tricky issues.'

'Go on.'

'Um ... might be better if we could meet up later. Talk it through. I know its short notice but I'd really appreciate it.'

'How about you pop round for a bite to eat at my place. I've got a few things to sort out, but let's say about eight pm.' She smiled at the hesitation from the other end. Knew Jackson's brain would be going into overdrive.

'Ok,' he finally agreed. 'Eight it is. Thanks Trish.' He put the phone down.

Trish sat there, thinking. Then she rang through to her PA. 'Alice, get me Art on the phone will you.'

The second ambulance pulled away from the sidewalk. No siren needed. The Police Officer was dead. His colleague had been taken to hospital an hour ago. Sedated and off for treatment, but not before McClure had spoken to him. Jackson arrived at the house on George Street just as the ambulance left. He got out of the car. Forensics were packing stuff away into their van. There was an air of sorrow over the scene. Cops downcast, not saying much. Eventually the teams began dispersing. Jackson ducked under the police tape across the front door and walked into the house.

'McClure?'

'Upstairs chief.'

It was quite a large property. Surrounded by shrubs and trees on three sides, it was fairly secluded. The downstairs was quite extensive with lounge, kitchen, dining room and large study. Upstairs were four bedrooms, two bathrooms and a second study room. It stood on a corner plot at the end of George Street and on the junction with Clifton Street, a spine road, which ran parallel with Baxter Boulevard and the curve of Back Cove. It was a bright cold day and the water in the bay looked liked a metal sheet under the cold November sun. The snow had come and gone.

Jackson climbed the creaking stairs, arrived on the landing and looked both ways. McClure peered out of a room down to his right.

'In here chief.'

The room was quite dark. A small shadeless light bulb struggled to make things any better. Jackson had expected to see blood and destruction, but the room looked surprisingly orderly.

'It's our guy. No question.'

Jackson nodded for McClure to continue.

'He broke one officer's arm very badly.'

'His name?'

'Carson. Mark Carson. The one killed is…'

'Jason Logan. I know them. They've been a team for long time.' They stood in silence for what seemed an age. Jackson kicked out at a bin and sent it flying to the other side of the room.

'God dammit McClure, what the hell's going on here.' He walked downstairs and out the front door. He asked a cop for a cigarette, lit up and drew the smoke deeply into his lungs. Blew it out and watched it spiral away into the crystal air. McClure came out and stood beside him.

'Chief.'

'Yup.'

'You gonna tell Logan's family?'

Jackson dropped the cigarette on the floor, stood on it. Looked up at the sky. 'I guess. Me and Jason go a long ways back.' They walked over to the car.

'McClure you get a lift back to the precinct. I'll go see his wife. Let's run a check on that clothing the John was wearing. I want you to handle that. Also get Blain to put a tail on that Pilkington guy — for all the good that'll do.'

'Ok chief.'

'Oh. And one more thing. Ring Art. I want a written report from him on the post-mortem with all that stuff he's told us about. I need it on my desk by…,' he looked at his watch. It was 3pm. '… 4.30pm.' The case was barely a day old and already he had a dead cop to add to the murder tally, two others attacked and a bunch of information from Art that sounded like it had come from out of a science fiction comic.

'No problem. Good luck with Mrs Logan.'

He walked off. Luck was the one thing in short supply just now. Especially for Jason Logan. Jackson rubbed the bridge of his nose, got in the car and headed up George Street.

Under the bridge that took *Route 295* above Sewage Plant Road was an area where the down and outs gathered towards the end of the day. They spent their time either congregating in nearby Loring

Memorial Park or scrounging amongst bins on the piers along the harbour. But by the end of the day they drifted back to the bridge. It was draughty but dry under there and at least they could hunker down at night without being bothered. Cardboard, old blankets and discarded clothes littered the ground. But they made perfect bedding.

At times some hobos stayed there all day. The old guy was there now. He was simply known as Whisky Mac. He had long, grey, greasy hair, a dirty bearded face with fierce blue eyes peering out from the grime. He always had cuts and bruises. He was always fighting with one or other of the drop outs so they left him pretty much on his own.

Whisky Mac had on two overcoats. But they still wouldn't keep him warm once the Maine winter set in. When younger, he would head a little further south towards Boston. But now with his aching body that sort of epic journey was beyond him. He'd survived two winters in Portland where temperatures locked below freezing most nights for at least two months and snow lay around until May. Last year was touch and go. He knew he wouldn't survive many more. As he lay in the darkness of the bridge, Whisky Mac heard something scuffling among the debris. He thought nothing of it. Probably rats, as usual. Then he became aware of the shape of a man against the blue sky beyond the bridge.

'Clear off. This is my patch.'

The man still came forward. He looked big, but that didn't bother Whisky Mac. He stumbled to his feet and squared up to the approaching stranger. 'Whadda you want?'

The stranger just pushed him to the floor, turned him over, and stripped his top long woollen coat off him, got up and walked off.

'Hey gimme that back, yer bastard.' But there was little venom in his threat.
Whisky Mac watched the man walk back out from under the bridge. 'Bastard,' he muttered again and fumbled around for some cardboard.

McClure had spent almost an hour at the store where the coat the dead man was wearing had come from. His initial query was met by an unhelpful shrug from an assistant. McClure eventually told him brusquely to fetch the manager. He certainly remembered the coat 'incident'.

'It was stolen from a rail there.' He pointed it out. 'There was quite a fuss. One of the staff spotted the thief looking at the coat, glancing round then calmly walking out of the store.' He had chased after him, shouting as the thief went out of the door, but once outside there had been no sign of him and, no, they didn't have CCTV.

McClure spoke to the staff member who had seen him, but given a frustratingly vague description. McClure was now relaying all this to Jackson back at the precinct.

'Did you get a description?'

'Yup, but not really helpful. One thing is for sure though, it wasn't the big guy. The thief was of a much slimmer build.'

'Could it be our John?'

'Not enough to confirm that chief, but I'm thinking it probably was.'

'So ... he stole the coat he was wearing. Now why would he do that?'

There was a brief knock on the door and an

officer came in. 'Excuse me Sir.'

'Broderick isn't it?'

'Yes, Sir.'

'What can I do for you?'

'Well, it's sort of about Kistner and Logan Sir. The guy who attacked them?'

'Go on.'

'Well, Sir yesterday we got a call to a food store in Cedar Street. Some guy went nuts in there when caught stealing food, injured one of the staff and got away. We filed a report before the end of our shift and then picked it up again this morning, talking to the staff, trying to get a description, that sort of stuff. Turns out they got cameras in there and got a shot of the guy. So we figured to get that out to catch him and close the case.'

'So what's this got to do with Kistner and Logan?'

'The thief Sir? He was a big guy. I mean big. And unusual.'

Jackson looked at McClure. Then back at Broderick.

'In what way unusual?'

'Well, he didn't speak or seem to understand English. He eventually said something, but it was a foreign language. That's not all either, one of the guys at the store said he had sort of yellow eyes.'

'You have the photo?'

Broderick pulled it out of a file and laid it on the desk. McClure walked round to look over Jackson's shoulder. The picture had captured the head and chest of the store thief. He had huge muscular shoulders, a powerful chest and large domed head with long dark hair plaited down his back. It was a sideways on shot. Broderick gave them another with the thief looking directly at the camera. It was a black and white but there was no mistaking a curious intensity in Crolin's eyes.

'You've done well Broderick. We'll keep these.'

'No problem, Sir. What shall I do ... about the theft from the store?'

'Proceed as normal. You will instigate a search for this man, but you are not to link him to the murder inquiry just now. Walk your own path and keep us informed of all developments. Is that clear?'

'Yes, Sir.'

'Oh, and Broderick, hold fire on releasing those photos. They're to stay under wraps for now.'

'Sir.'

After he'd left Jackson and McClure took another look at the photo. 'We need some more of these. Arrange that McClure.'

'Think that's our man chief?'

'Oh I don't have any doubts about that. But finding him is a whole different ball game.'

'Shall we put out an APB on him now?'

'Not just yet, not just yet.'

'But he's dangerous Sir. You forgetting he's killed two people now.'

McClure flinched as Jackson looked at him.

'I'm forgetting no such thing Sergeant,' he bristled. 'One of those he killed was a friend of mine or are *you* forgetting *that*?'

A heavy silence filled their office. After several minutes Jackson spoke again. There was an edge to his voice. 'McClure you're forgetting there's some mighty important points about this investigation that we aren't even close to understanding yet. If this ain't handled right some people are going to get spooked. Do you copy?'

'Yes chief.'

'We got any news from Blain on Mr Pilkington.'

'He hasn't left the hotel all day.'

'I'm also assuming we've nothing come back on the John yet.'

'Not a thing chief. It's like he didn't exist.'

Chapter 6

THE sky was clear, stars looked like chips of ice and, although no snow was forecast, temperatures were already in free-fall. It was going to be a bitterly cold night. Jackson drove over the Casco Bay Bridge with the Fore River a black sheen sliding under it. He swung round into Broadway and worked his way through the upmarket residential area to Glen Avenue. Eventually he pulled up into the driveway of Trish Longton's house. There were several big trees in the front, most of their leaves pooled in heaps of yellow and red at the bases. Jackson turned off the engine and sighed. This was dangerous territory, he thought to himself. It was only the second time he'd been out to her house. The first was just to pick up some paperwork. A door step visit. Now he was to go in. For a *bite to eat* as she had put it. He was wary of his own emotions.

Jackson walked up to the front door but it opened before he'd rung the bell.

'Hi, I heard your car.'

'Hello Trish.'

'Well, don't stand there, we're letting all the cold in.'

She closed the door and led him through the hallway. Wearing faded blue jeans with a wide black belt and simple white satin blouse she had the exact effect on Jackson that she had intended.

'Glass of wine?'

'Just the one, Trish. Firstly I'm driving, secondly I want to keep my head clear. This is going to be complicated.'

'I know,' she said over her shoulder as she walked off to get a bottle and two glasses.

He wondered what she meant by that. Her husband had worked in pharmaceuticals. They'd been married for 18 years until he died in an automobile pile-up on the way back from a conference in Boston. She had been devastated and had locked herself away with her grief; first into drink and then into work. It had been two years before Jackson was able to talk to her again and for the last four they had become good friends. He had been quite instrumental in helping her come to terms with life and these days she was a much more relaxed woman at peace with herself and the world.

'What do you know?' he asked as she came back.

Trish poured out the wine, went over to another coffee table. She picked up a document and dropped it into Jackson's lap.

'Art said he was sorry he couldn't get this 'til the end of play today. But here it is now.' She smiled and sat down beside him.

Jackson looked at the front of the document, looked at Trish and raised his eyebrows.

'Saves waiting for it until tomorrow.'

'And he knew I was seeing you tonight because...?'

She shrugged her shoulders. 'Makes for very interesting reading Jackson. Don't forget your wine.'

The 30-page document was thorough. It was in two sections. One outlying the key points, pretty much what Art had told the officers at their two meetings. The second went much deeper into the physiological aspects raised by the post-mortem. He started ploughing through the second section, but was struggling. After about ten pages he muttered something to himself.

Trish leaned over, rested her arm on his shoulder. 'I wouldn't bother with all that Jackson, you won't learn much from it that you need to know. Let's go eat.' She got up, leaving traces of her gentle perfume lingering in the air around Jackson.

He went through to the dining room. During daylight the large picture window framed a beautiful view of woodlands stretching to the hill at the edge the sea. Tonight it was pitch black with just a few terrace lights pulling nearby shrubs out of the dark. Jackson looked at the spread on the table. There was a bowl of spaghetti bolognese, plates of cold meats, cheeses, salads and several dishes of dips along with rolls, crisps and bowls of nuts and olives.

'This is a bite to eat?'

'Well, I'm guessing you haven't been concentrating on your eating today Jackson. Secretly he was pleased with the spread. Jackson was hungry. She topped up his wine glass. He didn't object. She was chatting about her work and the upcoming conference. It felt like they were skirting around the main business, but Jackson wasn't in a hurry. They went on to talk a little about their social lives and both relaxed into the evening.

'So,' said Trish eventually, 'This report makes for interesting reading. I've never heard of anything like some of that stuff Art has dug up.'

'Nobody has. And that makes things worse. It's really screwing up the investigation. Me and McClure can't get our heads round it. This stuff is hanging over us like some sort of weight.' He let out an irritable sigh. 'I don't expect you to come up with answers Trish. I just needed someone to bounce it off really. Help soak it up.'

'Let's go through to the lounge.' She switched off the dining room lights and they sat together on one of the sofas.

'Let me ask you a question, Jackson. What is the single most important thing you need to accomplish just now with this investigation?'

'We need to find the killer and get him convicted.'

'Right. And how's that going?'

'Well, we had a bit of a lucky break today when

a cop on another case came up with a CCTV snap of him.'

'So that's where your energy and work goes Jackson.'

'How do you mean?'

'This stuff with the double hearts and colour changing skin or whatever, as I see it that's not really central to your investigation just now. It may actually never be. But I understand how important it seems to be because of the very nature of what's been found.' Jackson was silent. 'You have two dead people. Almost certainly killed by the same person. You have a shot of him. That's what you focus on Jackson. The killer, not the victim. Once you get the former then the latter falls into place. That's what you're employed to do.'

'I've missed that part. Dammit you're right.' He rubbed the bridge of his nose. 'That's just what I needed to hear, Trish.'

'Of course how you go about that is up to you.' She smiled. It was getting late and he needed to head back to his apartment. Jackson stood, felt his head spin a little and realised he'd drunk more than he meant to.

Trish stood in front of him, a good head shorter. She reached up and put a hand on each shoulder.

'Thanks Trish that's been a real great help. My turn to treat you to dinner, maybe next week sometime?'

She regarded him steadily with her grey eyes. 'Oh Jackson what *am* I going to do about you?'

'Huh?'

She kissed him long and hard. It awoke something urgent in them both.

He had found one empty house. It shouldn't be a problem finding another. Crolin's almost animal instincts were on high alert as he prowled down Scott Street. An area of open back gardens between Frances Street and Edward Street cut off to his left. He made for some trees and shrubs half way along and then crouched down. He listened. And watched.

There were two houses without lights on. Crolin approached the first. Tried the back door, but it wouldn't give. He went round the side and looked through a window. There were signs of occupation. Furniture, ornaments. He slid away into the darkness and across to the other house.

He went through the same routine. This was one was practically empty, just a few pieces of furniture visible. It didn't look lived in. Crolin quietly forced the back door and went in. He shut it behind him, stood in the kitchen listening and then headed into the next room.

Something hit him. Hard. Knocked him to the ground. There was frantic barking and snarling. Strong jaws clamped round his wrist. It was a big dog and it was shaking his arm violently. It was a hell of a racket. Crolin rolled over on one side and hit the dog with his free fist. It gave a muffled yelp, but wouldn't let go. Crolin tried to roll away again, kicking over a chair and bin, sending them clattering across the floor.

He ended up wedged against the interior door. Which was just as well: on the other side another dog was barking loudly. Crolin could hear voices now outside the house. His blood was beginning to trickle on to the floor. He got up on one knee, lifted the dog off its front paws. The eyes were wild, almost rolled back into its head. Crolin hit it again, this time with full force. The dog yelped as it was sent spinning across the floor, but it came for him again.

This time Crolin was ready and as the dog lunged he spun away, slamming his massive forearm against the dog's neck. It was dead before it hit the floor.

By now someone was hammering on the front door and the second dog was howling on the other side of the kitchen door. Crolin raced out the back, cannoned into someone.

'Hey you, stop. Quick he's round here.'

But Crolin had fled into the night.

Jackson headed downtown. It was another cold crisp day. Hard blue sky, low bright sun and he knew he shouldn't be feeling good. Last night shouldn't have happened. But he smiled anyway. Trish had cooked him a good breakfast — bacon, beans, tomatoes, hash browns — the works.

He arrived in the office to find McClure busy putting together an incident board. In the middle at the top were a couple of the CCTV pictures of Crolin. Then shots of the victims and a map centred on the board with tapes leading out to the various photos and bits of papers. 'You been busy McClure.'

'Yes, chief. Figured we needed this now as we got a fair bit of info coming together. It's going to help us focus on our plan of action.'

'Good man. Sort of arrived at the same point myself last night.' He smiled.

McClure went off to get them coffee, wondering what had put his boss in such a relaxed mood this morning.

Jackson rang down to the front office and asked for any reports of overnight incidents to be sent up. After the store incident he wanted to keep close tabs in case their suspect surfaced again. It didn't take long to find out that he had. The break-in off Frances Street and scant description of the man concerned left him suspecting their man had been in trouble again. Jackson ordered the house to be sealed off immediately and sent a forensics squad down.

He went along the corridor to see if Blain was

in.

'Hiya, chief. Before you ask, our man didn't leave the hotel yesterday or last night. We have the place staked out this morning.'

That bit of information bothered Jackson on two fronts. Firstly he couldn't work out why Pilkington had stayed in most of the day and night and secondly what's to say he did. After all, given the stuff Art Williams had told him about the victim, it seems Mr Pilkington could have just melded into the background and walked.

As he headed back into his office McClure was laying some of the items returned by forensics on a table next to the incident board. He picked up the object he'd found at the alley. 'Boss, do you think it might be an idea if Lisa had a good look at this now?' He held up the bag.

'Sure. Can't do any harm.'

'Ok I'll go see her now.' He paused by the doorway. 'By the way any news on our man at Harbor View?'

'Seems like he stayed in.'

'Don't you think we ought to talk to him now?'

'I have that planned for later this morning. So don't hang around Lisa too long eh.' He winked.

McClure walked out shaking his head. What had got into Jackson this morning?

His mind was made up. But he had to be smart with his strategy. The key was staying in control of events. Mr Pilkington walked away from the window, picked up his coat and left the room. Once outside he smiled as he saw the tail in the car across the street. But he had nothing to hide and set off. He needed information from the cops and there was only one way of getting it.

McClure waved the bag in front of Lisa's face.

She smiled. 'Well, McClure aren't I a lucky girl. You could have brought me boring old flowers or chocolates. And what do you give me? Some strange object in a plastic bag.'

'Well, you know me, a romantic at heart.'

'So am I actually going to be able to hold this thing that's causing you so much of a headache?'

'Yup. Forensics have finished with it.'

'Did they come up with anything?'

'Big fat zero. No prints and no idea.'

Lisa took it out of the bag and was quite surprised at how smooth it was. She held it up to the light, then squinted at the edges. It was certainly lighter than a quarter. She put it under the magnifying table's glass and switched on the light.

McClure leant over her shoulder to get a look. 'What's all that stuff? Looks like writing.'

'We're not sure, to be truthful Sam.'

'We?'

'Yes, we. I ran the photos past three of the other conservators. We've not got very far. The scroll work is nothing any of us have seen before and the hieroglyphics look similar to stuff from ancient Egypt, but that's as far as we can tell.'

'Are they Egyptian?'

'Nope, just similar.' Lisa took the object out, inserted it upright into a special tray and then slid it back under the glass. 'Now this is what interests me.'

'What?'

He didn't get an answer straight away. She turned it over onto another edge and then again quietly murmuring to herself.

'When I looked at the photos the edge of this looked strange. It looked more than just being knurled like some coins are. It seems I was right. Look at this.'

He bent close to the glass and peered at it.

'The thing is, I thought they looked like the sort of cuts and edges you get on a key. And they are after a fashion, but with a slight difference.' She got a tiny pair of tweezers and started prodding at the edge. 'See, they move. You can push them in. Let go and they come back out. It's actually very intricate. Whatever it is.'

'You can't tell me any more?'

'Sorry Sam. This is beyond our expertise.'

'Well, thanks for your efforts, Lisa.' He started heading out the door.

'Sam.'

'Yup?'

'You still up for dinner next week.'

'Of course. Probably Tuesday, I'll call you.' And with that he was gone. She wasn't pleased, actually disappointed.

Jackson looked at the clock. It was just gone 11am. He really needed McClure back soon. There were things to do. His phone rang. It was front office.

'Yes, what is it?'

'There's someone here asking to see you Sir.'

'Well, I'm pretty tied up, can you get Blain to take it on?'

'Hang on Sir.' Jackson could hear a conversation going on in the background. 'He's quite insistent Sir. Says his name is Mr Pilkington.'

For any twists and turns in the investigation that might have taken Jackson by surprise, this was probably the biggest. 'Ok, Sergeant. Show him into one of the comfortable interview rooms. Make sure he has a coffee or tea if he wants one and tell him I will be with him shortly.

He put the phone down, stared at it and thought. After a few minutes he rang upstairs to Rotsko and gave him the news just to bring him up to speed. Then he rang McClure's cell phone to find out where he was.

'Just pulling in now chief.'

'Get up here fast.'

Jackson sat back in his chair and cast his eyes over the incident board. 'So Mr Pilkington. Where do you actually fit into all this?' McClure arrived several minutes later.

'Chief?'

'We have a visitor downstairs. A one Mr Pilkington. He's asked to talk to me.'

'Here?'

'Close your mouth McClure, yes here.' Jackson got up, grabbed a folder off his desk and headed for the door. 'You may as well come too.'

They went down to the ground floor, walked through the interview room door and McClure shut it behind them. Mr Pilkington was sitting on a low chair by the coffee table.

'Mr Pilkington. I'm Detective Jackson and this is Detective Sergeant McClure.' He held out his hand.

The man stood up, shook hands firmly with both officers. 'Pleased to meet you gentlemen. Thank you for seeing me.' There was no hint of an American accent. Probably English, but not quite.

Jackson couldn't place it.

'Sit down,' Jackson gestured to the chair and he and McClure sat on some chairs opposite. This was the friendly interview room. A non-confrontational room, as Jackson like to call it. Those were further down the corridor. In the back of his mind he wondered if they would have to move him down there at a later stage.

'I know you have been taking, how shall I say, an interest in me and my movements. So I thought we ought to clear some things up.'

Jackson liked that: straight to the point. The almost black eyes regarded him steadily. Not quite hostile, not quite friendly. But there was an unmistakeable intelligence there.

'Well, I might say the same of you Mr Pilkington.' Jackson put his folder on the table. 'You seemed to be taking a close interest in our activities at the alley off St Lawrence Street a couple of days ago.'

Mr Pilkington smiled and nodded. Almost to himself. 'Well, let's just say it involved someone I had a particular interest in.'

'Would that be the victim or the culprit?'

Mr Pilkington smiled again. 'I like you Detective Jackson. A man after my own heart. Cutting straight to the heart of things.'

Jackson became wary. He wasn't about to get sucked into a mutual back patting session with someone who might be a key witness –- or suspect — in the case. So he just nodded.

Mr Pilkington sensed the reticence. 'Maybe it would help if I cleared something up first. I'm sure you possibly suspect Mr Pilkington is a sort of alias.'

'Right. And your real name?'

'Ravenhart.'

'I see. And your full name, Mr Ravenhart?'

'That's it. Just Ravenhart.'

Chapter 7

CROLIN had spent the night hunkered down in a small parkland called Deering Oaks. Although they had lost all their leaves, the trees still provided enough cover. In the early hours, before first light, he'd set off hunting for another empty property. There were a lot about. He eventually broke into a vacant condo in Sherman Street. The place had recently been done up. The walls in the three rooms were pristine white with new, bare, wooden floors. The lack of heat didn't bother Crolin.

Stealing things was now part of Crolin's life. He felt it was beneath him, but necessary to survive. Apart from the mess-up in the food store he'd managed to get away with it. Now he needed to venture out on another gathering trip. By 11am he was back at the condo with food, a better overcoat – Whisky Mac's had stank – and shirts he ripped up to strap up his wrist. The bleeding had stopped quite quickly last night, but the wounds from the dog were sore and he needed to protect them.

Then Crolin started making plans to trap the hunter.

'So, just how can you help us, Mr Ravenhart?'

'Do they call you Mr Jackson?' There was a faint smile. Jackson barked out laughing. He couldn't help himself.

'So just how can you help us Ravenhart?'

'There's a lot of stuff to explain, but not all of it is going to be helpful straightaway.'

'You need to let me be the judge of that.'

Ravenhart realised he would need to play his cards a little closer to his chest. Jackson was sharp, but if Ravenhart was to control how things developed from here on out he would have to be a bit canny. 'Fair point.'

'So why were you watching us at the crime scene?'

'I'm assuming you haven't got an ID on the victim yet?'

Jackson shook his head. 'It is proving a problem.' The detective rubbed the bridge of his nose. 'Can you give us a moment?'

'Of course.'

Jackson and McClure left the room and went down the corridor.

'What's going on here chief? It feels like this guy is drawing us into collaboration instead of being questioned as part of the investigation. Let's get him in one of the main interview rooms.'

'That would be the obvious course,' said Jackson. 'But this isn't straightforward is it?'

'Yes it is!' McClure was beginning to get heated. 'This is a police investigation. We follow our usual procedure. There's nothing out of the ordinary here that needs concern us just now.'

'But that's just where you're wrong. His coming in here has derailed our normal lines of progress McClure. He is different.'

'He's just a man chief. Just someone who took an unhealthy interest down St Lawrence Street. Someone who is connected to this murder.'

'He isn't just a man though is he McClure?'

The breakthrough for Detective Doug Blain came at about the time Ravenhart walked into

Portland precinct. It was the one case which had given him huge problems at the start, but that was a little over three months ago now. It had been sitting on the shelf since then. Case still open, but unlikely to go anywhere. The woman's body had been found just off Maine Turnpike in Riverton. It was lying in scrubland wedged between the main route and Castine Avenue. It was discovered by a couple of boys who had eventually been told off by the parents for venturing nearer the turnpike than was good for them. They were just being boys. But the shock of the dead woman had traumatised them both. They may have been ten, seen plenty of violence on TV but this was the real thing. Fortunately for the boys there was nothing messy.

The woman was thought to be in her late 40s or early 50s, was still dressed — in plain skirt and blouse — there was no obvious cause of death. The post-mortem had revealed light bruising around her throat where someone had gripped her. There had clearly been some sort of struggle. But nothing obvious to cause her demise. Despite an intensive investigation, no ID had been established. Doug

Blain had hit a roadblock and, as other cases began piling up on his desk, the 'Riverton murder' eventually slid down the order. Jackson finally told him to just leave it as an open case, but to put no more time in on it. Then came a phone call that morning.

Maine is the most northern and eastern state of America. Much of it is wild and rugged, especially where it borders Quebec in the northern Appalachian Mountains. It is a harsh place, especially in the fierce winters. There are pockets of communities that can get locked in for months. Further round to the east, where Maine butts up against New Brunswick, the land is laced with lakes and rivers. One of the two main towns is Caribou which sits on *Route 1* and has a small airport to keep in touch with the rest of the world. Dotted around are several smaller communities. One of them is called Woodland.

It was a note from the Caribou police which was now sitting on Blain's desk. Attached to it was a photo. It was the Riverton murder victim.

'I'm sorry about that. We just had to clear a few

things up.'

Ravenhart understood perfectly. The young Detective Sergeant probably wasn't flexible when it came to stepping outside the playing field. He knew the sort, some worked for him.

'Not a problem, Jackson.' He leaned forward in his seat. 'I'm in a position to move your investigation forward.'

'You are?'

'Yes, the victim's name is Sarmira.'

'You have a first name?'

'I'm afraid not.'

'Ok. Not a name I've heard before. McClure get on it. Let's get some info on him.'

Ravenhart wasn't about to let on that Sarmira would be on no database they had.

With McClure out of the room, the tension relaxed a little. Jackson leaned back in his chair and took a long look at Ravenhart. 'You're a very interesting man Ravenhart. There's a lot more to you than you're letting on just now.'

'That may be true of you too Jackson.'

'But you're more relevant just now,' he said.

'Naturally we had a post-mortem done on this Sarmira.'

'Naturally.'

'It's caused a few problems.'

'Such as?'

Jackson filled him in about the hearts, the fingerprints and the strange composition of his skin. 'My sergeant there,' he thumbed towards the door, 'reckons he's an alien.'

'And do you?'

'Well, I ain't sure about that sort of stuff Ravenhart. But there's bits of him that sure ain't human.' He let that hang in the air for a few minutes. Trying to gauge Ravenhart's reaction. There was none. This lanky stranger with shoulder length black hair and eyes that gave nothing away just sat there with a faint smile playing at the corners of his mouth.

'Bit like you really,' said Jackson. Still no reaction.

Ravenhart leant forward, picked his mug of tea off the low table in front of him, sat back and drank, watching Jackson over the rim.

'You see the thing is, Ravenhart, I'm not sure

where this Sarmira came from and I also suspect that McClure is on a futile search for info on him just now. But I think you and this victim come from the same place.'

'Interesting deduction Jackson, but what if I say you're driving up the wrong track there.'

'Then you need to explain this to me.' Jackson picked up the folder and dropped the picture of Ravenhart — well half of him — on the table between them.

He picked the photo up and looked at it, nodding his head slowly.

'And while you're thinking up an answer you might like to explain how you just vanished right in front of me and McClure when we were tailing you up Pearl Street?'

Ravenhart made a decision. Jackson could see it in his sudden change of demeanour; no longer the man relaxing languidly in the chair. His face hardened, he sat forward. 'Ok Jackson this is the way it goes. There is something big cracking off on your patch. And you're right, we're not from round here. So I need to fill you in, but there's a deal to be done. Well, a couple actually.'

'We don't do deals, Ravenhart. We're police and we're investigating two murders and you will be co-operating with us. That's how it goes.'

Ravenhart shook his head. 'Fraid not, Jackson.'

Jackson stood up. 'I could read you your rights right now and we could haul your ass down the corridor and spend a long time asking you a lot of questions.'

'It'll get you nowhere Jackson and what's worse, I can be out of here, out of Maine, in a blink of an eye and you'll be left with a case that you'll never solve. Ever.'

Jackson sat down again. Behind the force and sincerity of Ravenhart's argument he saw the man was right.

'Ok so what's the deal?'

'Listen Jackson, I like you. We're not a lot of different in the way we operate. We actually do similar jobs,' he held up his hand as Jackson went to speak, 'but I'll tell you more about that later. The fact is that between us we will sort this out and sort it quickly.'

'So?'

'So there are some difficult things I need to tell you. Not difficult for me, you understand, but things that are going to be difficult for you to grasp and deal with. It is not information for you alone.'

'I'll get McClure back in here then.'

'Maybe at some point because he's pretty integral to all this, as is your sergeant. First off I need to meet with you and at least one other person you trust and respect. Someone who is not going to be phased by things outside, what you call, the ballpark. They also need to be experienced in police work. A good nose and good track record.'

It didn't require any thinking on Jackson's part. 'There's only one man that fits all that Ravenhart; Brett Rotsko. He's the Assistant Chief of Police; likes getting his hands dirty and did some good stuff in Cincinnati before he came to Portland.'

'Good. You need to get that set up. And the sooner the better.'

'I'll try and organise it for this afternoon. Tell him its absolute priority. Is that the deal?'

Ravenhart laughed at loud. It was an almost musical sound. 'You know it isn't Jackson.' He grunted. 'The deal is that a specially selected team is put together for this case from here on out, because there's stuff we're going to have to keep under wraps.'

'Well, once we've talked to Brett I guess that won't be a problem.' Jackson knew what was coming.

'And of course I'll be part of that team.'

Blain's office looked like a hurricane had gone through it. Outside the door stood a table piled up with files and books brought out from the room. All superfluous for the time being. One wall had been cleared and already an incident board was being set up. The victim's photo was at the top. And at last she had a name: Sally Johnson. On a nearby desk stood three boxes of files that two other officers were unpacking. There were photos of the crime scene, photos of the body, three folders which were the result of fruitless interviews, a box containing jewellery retrieved from the body and various reports from forensics and the path lab. Blain had put a call into the officer up in Caribou who had sent out the original APB report, but he was out on call and wasn't expected back for several hours.

'Let him know we have a possible ID on the bulletin he put out and get him to ring me as soon as he's back in town.'

As McClure came down the corridor he was aware of the sudden frantic energy buzzing around Blain's office. He knocked on the door frame and looked at the apparent mayhem.

'New case Sir?' he asked the detective.

'Ah, Sergeant. Where's Jackson?'

'Got someone in the interview room.'

'Ok. Let him know it looks like we've got an ID on the woman we found up at Riverton in August. The case is back on track again.'

'Great. How'd you get the breakthrough?'

'APB has come down from Caribou. She lived up that way apparently.'

'And it's taken them over three months to widen the search out over the whole of Maine? Boy those guys are slackers.' He headed off back downstairs.

The sticker on Blain's phone told him that he'd missed the call from the cop in Caribou; Sean O'Brien. It was not a part of Maine that Blain had ever ventured into and he had no plans to start now. He dialled the number. 'Hi, is that O'Brien?'

'Sure.'

'This is Detective Doug Blain. How you doing up there?'

'Not bad thanks. We've had our first snow, but don't think it's going to hang about too long just yet. Desk Sergeant tells me you got something on Sally Johnson.'

'Bit more than that. We have her body.'

'Oh damnation. Since when?'

'Since August. We found her on some land just off the Maine Turnpike outside the city. A place called Riverton. We spent a while trying to get an ID, but came up with zilch so the case has been pretty well shelved for at least a month.'

'How'd she die?'

'The cause of death isn't actually clear. There

was some measure of violence so it's down as a homicide. But how come you only just got a wire out on her.'

'Well, she was only reported missing three days ago. Thing is she lives in a small place some way outside Caribou called Woodland. Lives — or rather lived — on her own. Had a few horses and livestock, but kept pretty much to herself as the few folk up there do.'

'Who reported her missing?'

'Well, seems she has a daughter. Lives up by the river at Fort Fairfield.'

'Don't know it.'

'No reason you should. It's only a small town near the New Brunswick border. And the pair of them didn't seem to be in contact that much. Anyway it seems she told her daughter late July that she was heading West for a couple of months.'

'Holiday?'

'Sort of. She was hooking up with some old college friends in San Diego. It's where she's from originally. Sally told her daughter she would send her a card and be back at the end of September. There's been no card, her mum hasn't come back and so after leaving it for a few weeks in case she'd decided to stay on, the daughter came to see us. Really worried obviously.'

'Gee I'm sorry Sean. It's not good news.'

'Nope. I figure she may take it hard even though they weren't that close. Can you send me what you got on the case.'

'Sure the files are still here in my office.' He looked at the pile of stuff on the table across from his desk. 'You better get going your end and hopefully we can get some sort of breakthrough. You going to be the Case Officer?'

'Possibly, but I'll need to check with my chief now it's a homicide.'

'Let me know as soon as possible then Sean. Then maybe we can open up new lines of inquiry here depending what you got your end.'

'Sure thing bud.'

Blain rattled out an interim note and then mailed it through to Jackson to give him an early heads up on the developments.

He had no idea which hunter had been sent after him. Some were to be feared more than others, but when you were the one set in the sights then you wanted to keep out of the way, whoever it was. Crolin realised the hunter may well have the first part of the key, but he certainly wouldn't have the second that Crolin lost in the alley otherwise he wouldn't be sitting here now. He'd be in a very different and extremely uncomfortable situation.

Of course who did have the key was another worrying question, but not critical just now. Hunted turning hunter. It made Crolin snarl briefly. Maybe he could swing things to his advantage — as long as he made no more stupid mistakes. He was going to have to be very careful, maybe even relegate any movements to the night. Maybe by taking to the shadows Crolin could control the game. 'First I've got to set a trap though,' he said quietly to himself.

He emptied the small leather backpack out on the floor. Then opened the larger of the two metal cases, the black one, and took out the device. He turned it over in his hand absent-mindedly while thinking. This device was the crux of the hunt. He would either stand or fall and unfortunately it didn't entirely depend on how he used it. It also depended on how the hunter interpreted things when it was activated.

He looked at the two lights, both off now. This could lead him straight to the hunter. But it could also lead the hunter straight to him. Crolin sighed deeply. He was about to engage in a very dangerous game of hide and seek. And there was only going to be one winner.

Rotsko sat at his desk absorbing the information from Jackson. 'So all we really have from this Ravenhart is a name he claims belongs to the victim?' Jackson didn't answer. It wasn't a question that required one. The assistant chief was merely voicing the information he was turning over in his mind. 'What did he say when you dropped the photo in front of him?'

'Nothing about it. That's when he kicked into his; *We got something big we need to talk about,* routine.'

'Hmm. What's your take on him?'

'I like him actually. As a person. He talks straight and gets on with things. Bit like you and me really. Beyond that though is a whole pile of stuff that I can't get my head round.'

'Make that *we*.' Rotsko was hooked.

'So I guess we lose nothing by hearing him out. He's not nuts if that's what you're driving at.'

'I was, but trusting your judgement. What time's he due in?'

'I said to be here at 2.30.'

Rotsko looked at his watch. Ten minutes to go.

'There's something else come up that you need to know about,' said Jackson.

'Go on.'

'The body of the woman we found out at Riverton in August.'

'Yes. It's shelved but remains open as far as I understand.'

'Well, the case is live again. We've got an ID. Cops up in Caribou put out a missing person brief this morning. Turns out to be our body; one Sally Johnson. I've got Blain on the case.'

'Keep me briefed on that one as well. Be good

if we could tie it up. Having those sorts of loose ends hanging around doesn't look good.'

Ravenhart arrived at the precinct bang on time. Jackson brought him up to Brett's office and made the introductions.

'Hello, Ravenhart. Interesting to meet you.' Rotsko smiled.

Ravenhart shook the outstretched hand. 'You too.'

They all sat down around the table in Rotsko's office. 'So tell me what you know.'

Ravenhart leant forward, arms on the table. The relaxed air he'd given off when Jackson first met him hadn't returned. There was a sense of earnestness — almost urgency — about his manner. 'I'm sure Jackson has filled you in on what I told him earlier. The name of the victim, the fact that there is a significant situation in your city that you've yet to learn about and that the way ahead is by putting together a hand-picked trustworthy team to help deal with it.' He paused. 'And that I would be on that team.'

'Yes, he told me all that and some of the

reservations he has and the fact that there's stuff on our files we're not even close to understanding,' said Rotsko.

'Of course and I'm sure I can help you begin to get to grips with that, but as I explained to Jackson you are going to have to do your best to suspend some of your belief systems. What's going on here will extend well beyond your comfort zones, Mr Rotsko.'

'I have a question.' Jackson fixed Ravenhart with a stare. 'Can you tell me what sort of authority you have to walk in here and seem to be on a level with us? As far as I can see you're just some member of the public involved in something that we're investigating.'

Ravenhart gazed at Jackson for a long minute. In his mind he was ordering the information he needed to share and what he needed to hold back.

'After all,' went on Jackson, 'We're the ones that have two murders on our hands. We're the ones that are paid to get the answers. We're the ones that've got to find the killer and get 'em jailed.'

'But you're also the ones with questions you

can't possibly answer. And you can't answer them without my help.' It was a simple truth that carried Jackson's argument to a standstill. 'I'm not simply a member of the public Jackson and deep down you know that.'

Rotsko decided to cut in at this point after sitting back and watching the exchange. 'Then I think the best thing, Ravenhart, if you're going to get fully on-side with us, is to start by doing a little explaining.'

'Ok that's fine. But I need to explain things in an order that will help you come to terms with some of the stuff I have to tell you.'

'So what about that photo? That seems like a good place to begin,' said Jackson.

'I will have an answer Jackson, but that's most certainly not the place where I will be starting. First thing you need to understand is that the three of us are definitely not from round here.' He smiled. 'We're all from the same place.' Ravenhart waited for the impact.

'Three of you?' said Jackson.

'Me, Sarmira and Crolin.' Ravenhart had put

himself smartly into the driving seat, it would probably take Rotsko and Jackson a little while to realise it. But that was the game plan. 'Crolin is the man who killed Sarmira and he is almost certainly the man who killed your officer. You will not find Crolin on any of your databases either.'

They both waited for Ravenhart to continue. Not trusting themselves to even begin to ask the right questions.

'I'm guessing you have quite a lot of questions going through your heads right now, so let's try and clear some up.'

He got up and walked to the window which had an expansive view of downtown Portland. 'Where you live is an interesting place. Take this state. The landscape is very varied and you experience extremes of weather through the year. Take the planet as a whole and those things are magnified. So over billions of years you have evolved to adapt successfully to live here.'

'We're not here for some scientific history lesson, we're busy.' Jackson was getting edgy and it showed as impatience.

'Please, give me some room here. Where I come from is light years from here. I mean that in the literal sense.' Ravenhart turned round to look at them. To gauge their reaction. Rotsko was studying him steadily, weighing up; the man and the information. He was already thinking outside the box, thought Ravenhart. Jackson sat there, mouth hanging open.

Chapter 8

BLAIN'S phone rang.

'Hi.' It was Sean O'Brien. 'Just to let you know that I'm taking the case up here.'

'Good.'

'You also said to let you know of all developments?'

'Sure Sean. You got something in the first 30 minutes?' He chuckled softly.

'The forensics team have arrived at Sally's place. It's been turned over. I mean really turned over.'

'So what's that telling you?'

'Not sure at this point. We know she left on the flight down to Portland no problem so it happened after she left.'

'Ok.' Blain was just about to hang up.'

'It's not a robbery Blain. Firstly stuff like that happens once in a blue moon up here and secondly there's nothing missing. Someone was looking for something.'

Blain was intrigued, but only as far as a cop was intrigued. There was nothing in what Sean told him to tie the homicide into Portland. And that's what he needed to wrap it all up.

The air in Rotsko's office had gone very still. It was Jackson who finally broke the tension. 'You got to understand Ravenhart, I'm not a stupid guy, but I'm having a problem getting my head round this just now,' he said. 'You're sitting there telling me you don't come from this planet.' He rubbed the bridge of his nose vigorously. 'I'm a down-to-earth guy. I don't believe in ghosts and aliens.'

Ravenhart laughed. 'I'm neither of those Jackson. Face it, I'm not a lot different from you, am I? Just a couple of physiological differences. But evolution has dealt us a pretty similar deck of cards wouldn't you say.'

Jackson grunted.

Rotsko finally joined the conversation. 'Well, let's try and move it on a bit. At this point let's just accept what we're hearing Jackson. We have a murder case to deal with and it seems to me

Ravenhart is going to be some help.'

'I can see that chief, it's just there's bits of my brain being scrambled at the moment. God knows what McClure's going of make of this.' Jackson got up and poured himself another coffee. 'So where do you come from and, more to the point, how the hell did you get here?'

'I don't think it's going to be immediately helpful to go that route at the moment.' He held up his hand as Jackson started forming a protest. 'Trust me. I will tell you, but first we have to find Crolin. That's our most pressing business.'

'I agree,' said Rotsko.

'I cannot emphasise enough just how dangerous he is.' As Ravenhart spoke Jackson felt a chill run up his spine. 'I know he has killed one of your officers, and how particularly difficult that is for you, but I will tell you this. You have seen nothing yet of what Crolin is truly capable of.'

'How do you mean?' asked Jackson.

'Although he comes from the same place as me he is different.' He paused, wondering how to phrase the next statement in a way the pair of them could understand. 'A different race from me. Let's leave it there for now.'

'You mentioned a team,' said Rotsko. 'Do we need to think about that now?'

'We need to move beyond thinking. We need to start doing things. And doing them quickly.'

'How many cops do we need on the team?' Jackson was already running some names through his head. Rotsko was also jotting down names on a pad.

'Well, to begin with it will be you two.'

'I'm not a field man these days Ravenhart. I'm a desk cop.' He grimaced at the phrase.

'You're going to need to get back in the field. To start with you're already on-side with this and we need someone with your policing skills.'

Secretly Rotsko was pleased.

'Apart from you two I would suggest your sergeant, Jackson, two officers and a forensics man is going to be important. One who knows what we're tackling and we're going to need him on the ground with us.'

'That'll be Bob Webber. He'll buy into this

without too much trouble,' said Jackson. 'Finding two cops who aren't going to freak out might be a bit tricky. We don't have psychological profiles on them all.' His barking laugh was more a release of the tension that had been piling up inside him than amusement at his own joke.

'What about the officers that have already been involved with Crolin. The partners of Logan and Kistner. Do you think they'll be up for this?' asked Rotsko.

'That may not be a bad idea,' said Jackson. 'They've already had a run-in with Crolin. Loey should be ok, I'll just need to check out on Carson, how he is after the loss of Logan.'

'What about Art Williams?' asked Rotsko.

'Who's he?'

'He's the lead pathologist who carried out the post-mortem on Sarmira. He may be useful when it comes to dealing with … um … physical issues outside our knowledge.'

Ravenhart nodded.

'We're going to need to get them together for a briefing. Tomorrow morning?'

'Sooner than that I think Rotsko,' said Jackson. 'If I catch Ravenhart's drift we have to get things moving here.'

'Hmm. Right, Jackson you sound out Carson straight after this meeting and also brief McClure. Then I suggest we pull the team together here at 7pm tonight.'

'Sounds good to me.' Ravenhart finally leant back in his chair. Satisfied with the way things were going. It sounded like a workable team. There wasn't going to be a problem with him taking the lead. And that was important. If he managed to capture Crolin alive he needed to be in a position to get him away before anyone else realised what was going on.

The first thing Jackson actually did when he got back to his office was ring Trish. It was now into the afternoon and he realised he hadn't even spoken to her. He had her direct line. 'Hi Trish. I meant to ring earlier but the day has been crazy in more ways than one.' He heard her soft laugh on the other end of the line.

'Jackson I wasn't expecting you to call me, but

it's good to hear you.'

He hesitated. 'This is going to sound all wrong, but I need to talk to you again.'

'Are you trying to take advantage of a girl?'

He was pretty sure she was teasing him, but wasn't completely confident. 'No, no. Not at all. If you're busy …?'

She cut him short. 'Of course. Do you want to come round again?'

'If that's ok with you? We have something on here at seven, not sure how long it'll go on, maybe an hour.'

'I'll see you when you get here. Oh and Jackson …'

'Yes?'

'…bring an overnight bag this time.' She hung up before he could reply, smiling to herself.

Jackson looked at the dead phone and felt himself blush. Then he began wondering where McClure had got to.

At that moment he was back at the museum talking to Lisa. The pair of them were sitting at a table in one of the work rooms, surrounded by lumps of rocks and bits of pottery. She had phoned him to say she had emailed copies of the photos to a contact of hers in Boston. They were specialists in the field of Egyptian hieroglyphics and had actually got back to her with something.

'So what's your Boston buddy come up with?'

Lisa laid a photo on the table. 'There are seven hieroglyphs curving above the symbol in the centre.'

'How do you know they're above and not below? That scroll work might be the top.'

'True, but Patrick — he's the Boston buddy — recognised two of the hieroglyphs. So we know which way up they're supposed to be.'

'What about the other five?'

'He's not seen them before. But these two are interesting apparently.' She tapped the second and fourth ones. Then ringed them with a red felt pen. 'They both relate to creatures. This first one represents *Bastet*. She was a goddess of home that they worshipped for protection. This one here, however, is very interesting.' She paused. 'When are we having dinner again?'

'What? Oh.' He grinned, 'Tomorrow?'

'Good. So this one here is the sceptre of the scorpion. This creature represents a powerful force, but not for good. It was destructive and the interesting fact about this,' she tapped the hieroglyph with her pen, 'is that there is some sort of crossover with Greek mythology. The scorpion was represented by a similar symbol. It was also a powerful dark force.'

'Does that actually get us anywhere?'

'Well I guess it doesn't help your investigation very much, but Patrick was able to make a stab at what the combination of hieroglyphs stood for.'

'And that is?'

'It's some sort of call for protection against this.' Again she tapped the second hieroglyph. 'He also reckons that this main symbol in the centre represents some sort of gap, an entry or exit point. Probably one that could be used for good or evil.'

'How the hell does he arrive at that conclusion?'

'Patrick has spent 40 years working in this field. His conclusion is built on a profound depth of knowledge. I tell you Sam, that's probably the best and soundest interpretation you're going to get.'

'But what is this object actually for?'

'That we're not sure about. But it seems similar to the keystones you have in Egyptian tombs. It is probably used to insert in something to unlock it.'

With McClure out of the office, Jackson decided to talk to Carson. After the death of Logan he had been signed off on compassionate grounds so he drove out to North Deering where he lived. After the preliminary, *How you doing buddy?* Jackson got to the point. He judged that Carson had been naturally rocked by the death of Logan but he wasn't emotionally unstable. Indeed getting back to work might actually do him a power of good.

'The thing is, Carson, that the case is beginning to shape up and, as you've already had a run in with the killer, I want you on the team. You've had first-hand experience of him.'

'I can handle that Sir.'

'We now have a name and some more information that's going to move it all forward.'

'Who is it Sir, I may know him.'

'You won't. Trust me. We're putting together a special team to deal with this. I want you in. You think you're up to it?'

'Definitely, Sir. I'm going to go stir crazy if I sit around here until someone decides I'm fit for service again.'

'Good man. The team's getting together tonight for the first briefing. It's at seven in Rotsko's office.'

Carson raised an eyebrow; 'He's part of this?'

'Very much so, but that'll all become clear later.' Jackson put his coat on as he walked down the hallway towards the door. 'Oh and one more thing Carson. This is all very hush-hush just now. We don't want to be spooking who we're after so we're playing it tight. Got that?'

'Yes, Sir.'

McClure was in the office when Jackson got back.

'So what you been up to McClure?'

The sergeant explained about his meeting with Lisa and what the man from Boston had said about the object. 'You know me chief, all seems far out. But the guy's a top class expert in it and that's what he came up with.'

'Good work.'

'Beats me why someone spends their life looking into all this sort of fantasy crap. They need to get real.'

Jackson sighed. The next ten or fifteen minutes were not going to be easy. 'I need to explain something to you McClure and you gotta try and listen without getting wound up.' Jackson got up, went over and closed the office door.

McClure watched him. Jackson never closed the office door. He wondered if he'd got himself in trouble. But he couldn't see where. Jackson sat down and leant back in his chair.

For the next ten minutes he explained to McClure what had taken place in the meeting with Rotsko and Ravenhart. It was at some point during this talk that a secretary walked past. Just as she noted how odd it was that Jackson's door was shut, a *You're fucking well kidding me!* exploded with force from inside.

Back at his hotel, Ravenhart was drawing up a plan of action. He was pleased with the way things had developed and hoped Jackson wasn't having too much trouble with his sergeant. That was one very sceptical man who was going to have his eyes opened — very wide.

Down in the lobby, Ryan was still dumbstruck that Mr Pilkington had smiled at him when asking for his room key.

Ravenhart opened the smaller of his two tan leather suitcases, lifted out the black box, opened it and put the gatetrap on the bed. He didn't need a key, unlike Crolin. Hunters had sole command of their gatetrap. It was a critical part of their tracking armoury.

McClure was still fizzing. He sat at his desk questioning the sanity of people, his life, the world and anything else that raged through his brain. It was dark outside and flecks of snow were caught in the light as they drifted past the window. He looked at his watch. It was almost time for the meeting —

and he didn't even know who was going to be there. McClure had wanted to ring Lisa but had been told in no uncertain terms by Jackson meeting that he was to say nothing to anybody.

'Frigging aliens,' he'd muttered as he walked out of Jackson's office. 'More like some fruitcake.' He popped his head back in the office. 'Nuts! The guy's just nuts,' he bellowed. He walked off.

By 6.30 Jackson was already up in Rotsko's office. 'How'd it go with McClure?'

'He's having a bit of a problem with it,' laughed Jackson.

'Will he be stable enough to be on this team?'

'Yeah. He'll set his problems aside and get on with the police work. I'll bet on that.'

They went through the plan for the evening's meeting as far as they could. But they were very much in Ravenhart's hands. Rotsko was suddenly aware they didn't know what sort of role Ravenhart had back home — wherever that was.

A short while later everyone was gathered round the table in Rotsko's office; Ravenhart,

Jackson, McClure, Webber, Loey, Carson and Williams.

'Right gentlemen,' said Rotsko. 'This is going to be a difficult evening for some of you. This is the operational team for finding the killer of the victim found in the alleyway off St Lawrence Street two days ago and of Officer Logan. It is difficult because the information you're about to hear is not only highly confidential and must not be talked about outside this team unless I say otherwise, but because it is also going to introduce aspects that you have never encountered before.'

There was a shifting in the seats and glances.

'The first thing I'm going to do is ask Art to go over the post-mortem results from the alleyway victim. It may help ease you into some of the more difficult issues.'

After he'd gone through the report, which was new to Webber, Loey and Carson, a hush settled over the room. Already Webber was ahead of the game concerning the potential implications.

'At this point I'm going to hand over to Ravenhart. He knows the victim and the killer and he's best placed to take things on from here.'

'My job,' he began, 'is not a lot different to what you people do. Where I come from we have people who get murdered, commit crimes of various sorts and so we have to deal with that. We do it a little differently, but we deal with it. We're not called police. We're called hunters.' He paused. No-one said anything. 'We don't have ranks as such like you, but hunters gain stature through their effectiveness. I am recognised as their most efficient hunter. And that's why I'm here in your city.' There was no hint of arrogance, just a cold, clinical certainty of his ability.

Webber spoke up; 'Where are you from?'

'Gamlin.'

'And where the hell's Gamlin?' This from McClure.

'It's in a universe parallel to yours. In other words a long way from Portland.' Ravenhart wasn't smiling when he said it.

'Sir, is this guy for fucking real?' McClure directed his appeal to Rotsko.

'At this point in time, Sergeant, he is. We have two murders and a man standing here who knows the killer and one of the victims. You'd better believe it's real. And that goes for all of you.'

'So how did you get here? As I understand it those who believe in parallel universes say travel between them isn't possible,' said Webber.

'There are not many of you who even believe in parallel universes. But the mode of travel from Gamlin to here is not going to help you just now. You've enough to get your heads round.'

'People, we need to try and treat this as a straightforward murder case as best we can. I know some of these issues are uncomfortable, even unbelievable,' Jackson looked at McClure, 'But the fact is we need to get this wrapped up.'

'The victim's name is Sarmira.' Ravenhart hit a laptop button and the victim's picture came up on the screen, 'And his killer's name is Crolin.' The CCTV picture from the store flashed up. They came here from Gamlin together. It was an unauthorised trip. Crolin is a wanted man back there. He is a killer. Sarmira was an authority figure. He was what we call a *gatekeeper*.'

'What does he do?' asked Rotsko.

'His job is basically to control travel to and from Gamlin. To anywhere. Within our solar system, galaxy, universe or, as in this case, parallel universes.'

'Plural?' said Webber.

'Oh indeed. But let me get to the point. Crolin was banned from using gatekeepers so forced Sarmira to open the gateway to your planet.'

'How did you find out he'd gone and where to?' asked Jackson.

'Well, obviously Sarmira's disappearance triggered the alarm and once we realised that we used the information on our gate database to track Crolin's destination.'

'He killed Sarmira?'

'He did, but that is a puzzle. He'd need Sarmira to get back to Gamlin. He couldn't do it on his own.'

'Maybe he didn't want to go back,' said McClure.

'Possible, but unlikely.'

'Well, if he's in trouble there, why would he not stay here?'

'He'd be way out of his comfort zone in terms

of language and culture. Also because of his particular physiology he wouldn't survive here much longer than two years.'

'That's interesting. I didn't pick up anything like that from the post-mortem,' said Art Williams.

'You wouldn't. He's not the same race as Crolin.'

'Ah. Now that *does* sound interesting.'

'So,' said Jackson. 'Crolin's our man. All we've got to do is catch him.'

'Agreed,' said Ravenhart, 'But let me tell you, this won't be a straightforward business. He is dangerous, he is a killer. We've spent a long time trying to nail him. He's a very smart animal.'

The team was to meet at 9.30am the following morning when a strategy would be planned out. Ravenhart headed back to his hotel, quietly satisfied that everything was holding together well. As they all left the office Rotsko asked Jackson to hang back. 'What did you make of it then?' asked Rotsko.

'Went pretty well, I'd say, considering. McClure's still on edge but he'll be fine.'

'And what else? I can read you Jackson.' He laughed.

'Ravenhart hasn't given us everything.'

'Well, maybe that's not a bad thing. We've got enough to get our heads around without learning any more about his world.'

'That's not what I mean. I'm talking about stuff that's relevant to our investigation. I think he's still holding out.'

'Hmm. But I've got to give him credit for the way he steered everyone through that.'

'Sure, but it's just a hunch.'

Rotsko made a mental note. Jackson was rarely wrong when it came to hunches. 'You want to stop for a drink on your way home.'

'I'll skip that Brett I've got somewhere else to go.'

Rotsko raised his eyebrows. 'You holding something back as well?' He heard Jackson's barking laugh as he walked off down the corridor.

He could hear someone sneaking round the back of his place. Crolin's senses were on high alert.

He moved silently to the window and looked down on the area round the back of the condo. It was black and snowing a little more steadily. He went downstairs, then heard the backdoor handle being rattled. Crolin wrenched it wide and someone yelped, but they weren't alone. It was a gang of youths and they were laughing at the one who'd been frightened.

'Hey come on out old man. What you doing in there, hobo?'

It was the pack mentality. Safety in numbers. So they were jeering at Crolin. Even his bulk didn't send out any alarm signals. As he stepped outside two of the gang closed in behind him. One pushed him in the back. Crolin turned and snarled, another pushed him again. Now they were having fun, laughing and jeering. Calling him names. Crolin didn't understand the taunts. Someone pushed him again from behind. He spun round and lashed out but the youth was already out of range. They were dancing around him, circling like a pack.

A pack. It fired the trigger. Something lashed out in the dark. Vicious. Lightning quick. The spike impaled a youth's thigh. His scream of pain ricocheted off the walls. Blood bloomed in the settling snow.

Once again Jackson was heading over Casco Bay Bridge, the wipers going steadily. Snow was coming at him out of the dark, like pin pricks of stars. He almost imagined he could be shooting at some warp speed through a galaxy. The thought took him back to the day's unfolding events. He was probably having as much trouble as McClure believing what he was hearing. He just didn't voice it in the same way. It was all churning around inside him. Suddenly every concept he had about life, his understanding of the order of things, had been blown completely out of the water. Jackson wasn't much into astronomy. The planets, the stars, galaxies, the universe. He just knew that it was all out there, that it was very big and very much beyond his comprehension. Now a completely new dimension had been introduced. And it wasn't just theory. He had spent much of the day talking and listening to somebody from a planet in a parallel galaxy — he still didn't understand that concept in any shape or form — and now he just had to accept it all. Jackson wondered what Trish would make of it. Knew he shouldn't even tell her, but knew he would.

McClure didn't know what to do with himself. His mind was in turmoil. He knew he'd lost it a couple of times today, but what the hell. That stuff just wasn't reasonable. He found himself in the Lobster Bar at Harbor View Hotel. Maybe subconsciously he was hoping to bump into Ravenhart. He was on his second Jack Daniels. Maybe he should ring Lisa. See if she was up for a drink on the spur of the moment. He pulled out his cell phone and rang her. By the time she arrived he was into his third. He bought her a drink and they settled down on a sofa in a corner at the back of the bar.

'So what's up Sam?'

'I've had a day you wouldn't believe.'

'Want to tell me about it.' She realised he was more than a little stressed out.

'Hell, I'd like to Lisa, but we're not supposed to

say anything in case we blow the operation.'

'Operation?'

'There you go, I've started already.'

She laughed. So he told her about a special team being put together to find the killer of the alleyway victim and the cop.

'So what's so hush-hush?'

He hesitated. 'You know that hieroglyphics stuff? About the entry and exit point; the symbol?'

'Yes.'

'Well it's nearer the truth than you think.' Then he fell silent.

'I have a bit more information, but I don't know how relevant it is.'

'Go on.'

'You know a lot of my background is in Native American Indian folklore?'

'Yup,' he said, glad to be steered away from saying something he shouldn't.

'Well, what Patrick told me about the symbols and what they represented was niggling away at me for a good part of the day. It was not long ago I realised what it was. Remember the symbol for the destroyer?'

'The sceptre of the scorpion – I liked that. Wasn't that the one that had some link to the Greek stuff?'

'Yes. Well, there's also a similar mythical creature in the Indian folklore. It's a *Kanaima* which is a vengeance spirit. And the interesting thing about this is that *Bastet* …'

'The good goddess.'

'…yes, one of her attributes is vengeance.'

'So what represents the *Kanaima*?'

'It isn't represented by anything. Tradition says that it is an evil spirit that possess people causing them to turn into a deadly animal and go into a murderous rage. Usually seeking revenge for a slain relative.'

Emotions were a funny old business, thought Jackson as he headed back downtown. It was a slate-grey morning with patches of the overnight snow lying around at the sides of the road. But it was disappearing fast as the temperature rose. As he swept once again over Casco Bay Bridge Jackson was in a reflective mood. Last night with Trish Longton had been very special — for both of them — but especially for Jackson. At a point in his life when he was facing something that had shaken him to his foundations, put him in turmoil, he had also found a safe harbour. In the wake of Ravenhart's revelations, suddenly all Jackson's worries and fears about stepping into a relationship he wasn't sure either of them wanted, were simply washed away. Last night was a new beginning for both of them.

For McClure too the shocks of the day had been a catalyst. It had mellowed him and Lisa found him in a strangely satisfying emotionally-pliable mood. They had stayed the night at his place. He'd said no more about his police work, though she knew that whatever it was had disturbed him greatly. He was different. She was under no illusions it would last, but maybe it gave them a chance. Which, deep inside, she realised she wanted.

At this point McClure, like Jackson, was heading into the precinct. And at this point both of them had begun wondering just what lay ahead in the day. It didn't take long to find out.

As soon as Jackson walked through the front doors the Desk Sergeant called him over and handed him a report from last night.

'Looks serious chief.'

Portland wasn't a violent city. Probably about 20 to 24 homicides a year at most. Now he was reading about a second one within three days. He was sitting at his desk scanning a report when McClure came in, much subdued.

'You ok, McClure?'

'I'm fine chief. I'm fine.'

'You better read this.' He held the report out for McClure. 'Looks like the work of Crolin again.'

The report was confused and rambling. A group of youths had been baiting what they said was a hobo off Sherman Street. Seems like he turned on them, put some sort of spike through the legs of one of them who he bled to death. They called the police but the attacker had run off into the night. Described him as a *big guy*.

'Might not be Crolin, there's more than one *big guy* out there.'

'True, but the reaction is a might excessive

shall we say?' said Jackson. 'The most aggressive
I've ever known a hobo to be when they're being
wound up is to chuck a bottle at their tormentors.
Making sure its empty first of course.'

'Want me to go out to the scene?'

'No, we've got our meeting soon. There's a
team down there and I've told them to keep us up to
date with anything they get. I'm not expecting much
to be honest.'

Rotsko had got into the office an hour earlier
and had already seen the report of the previous
night's incident. He had also spent his time trawling
through all the case work. Rotsko felt alive again;
getting his teeth into ground work. But there were
still too many questions. Why were these people
from Gamlin even here? Why did Crolin kill Sarmira?
Is Ravenhart going to settle for justice being dealt
with here or will he want Crolin taken back? He
suddenly laughed out loud at the thought of a court
having to deal with extradition to a parallel universe.

The team was gathered once again in Rotsko's
office and he was pleased to see that McClure

seemed much more relaxed. He briefed them all on last night's incident.

'Is that likely to be the work of Crolin?' he asked Ravenhart.

'I would like to know a bit more from the scene. It is very possible but a lot of the information in this report isn't that helpful.'

'Well, the kids were frightened and confused. It was dark, snowing and one was dying in front of the rest, so it's understandable.'

'It'll probably make them think twice about winding up a hobo, or anyone for that matter, in future,' said Carson.

Jackson grunted. 'There's a crime scene team down there now going over the area. My money's on Crolin. We've already chased him out of the Bay Cover area and this place isn't far from another disturbance in Frances Avenue which almost certainly involved Crolin.'

'He was probably holed up there somewhere,' said McClure.

'The thing is we keep breaking his cover which is no bad thing,' said Ravenhart. 'When he's under pressure like that he will make mistakes and then we can track him down.'

'Is there anything we can actually do?' asked Carson. 'It seems to me he appears then disappears and we get no trace. We're always behind the game.'

'I think the best thing is for me to get down to the scene and see what I can find,' said Ravenhart.

'I'll come,' said Rotkso. 'Carson and Loey I want you to question the other guys involved last night. McClure you go with them. Question them closely, go for every and any detail you can get, *however small*. It could be vital.'

'And me?' asked Jackson.

'I want you back here for now as a link man. Anybody gets anything it comes straight back to Jackson and we'll act as necessary off the back of that.'

'Hello Sean, how's it going up there?'

'Forensics have been through Sally Johnson's place. There's not much to be honest.'

Blain didn't expect much else.

'We found an envelope with six photos in. A picture of Sally and some guy. We showed them to her daughter, but it's no-one she knows.'

'You want me to take a look?'

'That's what I was thinking. There may be a Portland connection.'

'Fine, fire them down the line Sean.'

'There's one other thing. Seems like she didn't want these to be found.'

'How so?'

'There's some doors that open into the eaves in the top room. This envelope was taped to the top of a beam in there.'

'Your boys are thorough.'

'It's what they're paid for. The question it raises in my mind is, are these the photos wanted by whoever turned over her house?'

'I would say so, yes,' said Blain. 'Maybe it was whoever is in the photo.'

'That's the way I'm thinking. Thing is this seems completely out of character for her. She led a very quiet life up there in Woodland.'

'People will never stop surprising us Sean.'

'True. Right they should be with you now.'

'Thanks. I'll get back to you.' Blain called the photos up on his screen. He recognised her from the shots on the wall in front of his desk. He'd not seen the man before. The pictures were taken on the edge of woodland. Neither was smiling. He printed them out, pinned one up on the wall and left the rest on his desk.

Jackson was frustrated. Everyone was out doing something and he felt at a loose end. It had been over an hour since the morning meeting and nothing had come back yet. He wandered down to Blain's office to see how things were going with his homicide.

'Hi Doug.' He sat in the chair in front of the detective's desk.

'Jackson. How's it going? Looks like a bit of a buzz kicking off down your end.'

'Yup we got a team and had a couple of breakthroughs. We know who we're looking for, just gotta find him now.'

'Good, let's hope you nail that cop-killing

bastard soon. Who's the suit, by the way? Saw him when you were all on your way up to Rotsko's office.'

Jackson wasn't quite sure what to say. It hadn't even occurred to him that somebody would ask the question.

'FBI?' ventured Blain.

'Can't say too much just now Doug.'

'Surely not CIA?' Blain then laughed.

'So how's things with your case?'

Blain told him about the daughter and the ransacked house.

'It's probably the most excitement those guys have had up in Caribou for a while. I guess most of their stuff is traffic violation and misdemeanour offences. Coffee?'

'No, I'm drowning in the stuff.'

'Oh, there was one other thing. Sean O'Brien, the Case Officer, was on the phone not long ago. They found some photos of her with some dude and mailed them down. Just in case we knew him. It didn't ring a bell with me, but I've sent it round.'

'Well, I'll leave you to it. Let's hope those Caribou guys crack this and we can get it off our

books. I got too many homicides open just now.'
Jackson glanced at the incident board as he started
passing through the door, stopped and came back.
'Oh shit.'

'Jackson?'

'Oh shit!' He tapped the photo. 'Sarmira.' He
took it off the board and marched out of Blain's
office. Blain stared after him and looked back at the
gap in his board.

Chapter 9

ROTSKO and Ravenhart were standing in the empty Sherman Street condo.

'He was definitely here,' said Ravenhart.

'How'd you know?'

Ravenhart looked at Rotsko, his eyes steady, sure. 'I'm a hunter. I know these things.'

'There's nothing here anyway,' said Rotsko.

'No,' said Ravenhart, almost to himself. 'He'd have taken it with him.'

'Taken what?' Silence. 'Ravenhart, taken what?'

'Uh? His stuff.' It wasn't convincing, but before he could press further Rotkso's phone rang.

'Ok we're coming back right now.'

'What's up?'

'Seems we have an interesting line on Sarmira.'

'Oh. What's come up?'

Rotsko smiled. Two could play the evasive game. 'Let's go and see, eh?' With that he headed out of the condo.

The atmosphere was pretty electric. It was late afternoon and on the screen in Rotsko's office was the picture of Sarmira and Sally Johnson.

'Well at least it makes things a little more tidy for us here in Portland precinct,' said Rotsko.

'How so, chief?' asked McClure.

'Well, we got all the homicides in the same bag — for now anyway. Though I'm damned I can see a link.'

Blain had joined the case team after a long briefing from Jackson and Rotsko. Like the rest he couldn't comprehend properly the Gamlin angle and gave up trying pretty soon after he was told. It was a homicide case plain and simple as far as he was concerned. Ravenhart had remained quiet, thoughtful. He had nothing to offer on the link between Sarmira and Sally Johnson.

'Do we know where this was taken?' asked Jackson.

'I've been back to the boys in Caribou. They're trying to place it,' said Blain. 'As far as they're concerned we've got an ID on the guy and it ties him in with the case we've got down here. That's all I told them.'

'Which is about right,' said Jackson. 'Just leave Ravenhart and Gamlin out of the equation.'

'No problem there.'

'If this picture sources Sarmira up country, what the hell was he doing there?' asked Rotsko. 'Any idea Ravenhart?'

'No I haven't. There's nothing I know of that should have taken him up there.' He was deeply puzzled.

'Damn.' Jackson banged the table with the flat of his hand. It made them all jump.

'What, Jackson?' asked Rotsko.

'For the life of me I don't know why any of us hadn't thought of this before, but there is a big question staring us in the face that we haven't asked. A big question.'

Nobody said anything.

'Ravenhart, you haven't told us what brought Sarmira and Crolin here. We've been so sidetracked by the enormity of what you've told us, we've missed the simple stuff.'

All eyes turned to the slim man sitting at the end of the table. He returned the gaze, his black eyes with chips of light, unblinking.

'I've told you as much about Sarmira as is necessary at this stage.' There was a sharp edge to his voice.

'Ravenhart, that doesn't answer the question,' said Jackson. 'All we know is that you're hunting Crolin. Apart from telling us he's dangerous you haven't told us, specifically, why you're after him.'

'I also have another question,' said Rotsko. 'When we do get him, what happens at that point? Because we will want to bring him to trial. He has committed two, possibly three, homicides here in Portland and this is where justice will be delivered.'

Ravenhart was unbowed by the pressure. 'I have told you all you need to know.'

'That is not enough!' shouted Jackson. 'Remember this is our case.'

Ravenhart stood up. Looked around the table at the team, emanating a cold resilience. 'Then I wish you good luck.' And with that he walked out the room.

It was Rotsko who went after him. Caught him by the arm as he was about to enter the lift. He was surprised by the power in Ravenhart's slim frame as he violently shrugged the Assistant Chief aside. They stood staring at each other. Rotsko, puzzled, Ravenhart bordering on hostile.

'Let's go and talk somewhere quiet. Just you and me.'

Ravenhart gave a curt nod.

Rotsko closed Jackson's office door. 'You've got to understand that my people have had to take on board a lot of strange information. So have I come to that. We can't even begin to process it. It's all just sitting there in our heads like some unfathomable congealed mass while we're trying to deal with a growing murder count on our patch. It's not easy for anybody.'

Ravenhart gave a long sigh. Ran his hand through his hair. 'I'm aware of that Rotsko. That's why I don't want to feed them anymore than is necessary. They have valid questions and I can answer those later, but they are not important just now.'

Rotsko sensed there was more. And waited.

'I'm not a stranger to this.' He gestured around the office. 'This isn't the first time I've had to come here from Gamlin. Last time I explained too much. People couldn't handle it, the whole thing fell apart and after killing several people Crolin got away.'

'He's been here before?'

'Yes.'

'May I know where?'

Ravenhart thought for a moment. 'It isn't specifically relevant to this case and it would be helpful if we kept this between ourselves for now.'

It was Rotsko's turn to nod without comment.

'The best way I can put it is like this; on Gamlin we age differently to you. Crolin has actually come here a number of times over 200 years and killed a lot of your people. This is only the second time I've been the hunter they've sent after him.'

'When were you here last?'

'That would be about twenty years ago, that's all. I tracked him to San Diego. I would have actually had him if I'd handled your people slightly differently.'

'And that's why you're being cautious now.'

'Indeed.'

'I have one further question.'

'Go on.'

'Why is Crolin coming here killing our people?'

Ravenhart hesitated. It was a big question. It was *the* question. He decided that Rotsko was the right man to tell.

'It's all about vengeance.'

Rotsko felt a cold chill flood through him.

Blain arrived back in the office after the case meeting had broken up in a storm to find a large cardboard box dumped in the middle of his desk.

'What the hell's this?'

'Arrived this morning from Caribou. Some of the stuff they found at Sally Johnson's place.'

'Then you better start unpacking it Officer.' He lifted it onto the table next to the incident board. 'And don't forget to log it all.'

'There's a note on an envelope in here for you boss.' It was from Sean O'Brien;

These are the photos we found.

There was also some metal object in there with them.

Good luck.

Blain took out the photos and a small brass-coloured rectangular metal plate in a plastic bag dropped out. It was smooth on one side, had some sort of markings on the other and was slightly thicker than a coin.

'What the hell's that?' He held it up, inspected it closely and then went off to find Jackson. He tracked him down in Rotsko's office. But only he and McClure were left there.

'New office boys?'

'Seems like the chief is locked up in our room with Ravenhart. Tetchy bastard,' said McClure.

'He certainly is a strange one,' agreed Blain. 'I just got a box full of stuff over from Caribou including the photos. They were found in an envelope and this was in there as well.' He held up the bag.

McClure got up, looked at it and then took it off Blain. 'Well, I'll be.'

'What is it McClure?'

'It's got the same sort of symbols on it as that

other thing I found in the alley.'

Crolin had spent the rest of the night back in Deerings Park, sleeping deep in the shrubs. The youths had been stupid; didn't realise what they were awakening. He felt no pity or remorse for the one he'd killed. But he was hungry. The whole thing had sapped energy. He was going to have to risk being out during the day. This time, however, he'd make sure he'd get food without causing such a row. He also had a problem about being ousted yet again from a base. After making sure nobody would catch sight of him emerging from the parkland, Crolin set off up the road in his coat and sunglasses, a small leather pack on his back. Then it occurred to him that once police had finished with the Sherman Street condo it might actually be the smart place to go back to that night. They wouldn't expect that of him.

It was late afternoon when Rotsko called the team back together. Already it was getting dark outside and turning bitterly cold again. They were surprised to find Ravenhart there. He sat impassively, leaning back in his chair, completely relaxed. As if nothing had happened.

'Ravenhart and I have had a long chat to clear the air. He's told me a little bit more, but nothing that I need to pass on to you just now.'

'Chief?' Jackson was agitated.

'You have to trust me with this Jackson. And all of you. What he has said is of no immediate help to our main task and that is to find Crolin. You have enough to contend with for now.'

Jackson didn't like it, but ultimately made a grudging nod of acceptance. He would trust Rotsko with his life.

'Have we any idea if Crolin is likely to strike again and where?' asked McClure.

Rotkso looked at Ravenhart. 'He said it's impossible to say.'

'Why doesn't he just leave for Gamlin?'

'He can't,' said Ravenhart. 'Not without Sarmira and he's killed him. He's effectively trapped here. I'm the only one who can get him a passage home in a manner of speaking. He knows a hunter is here, he doesn't know who or where.'

'So why did he kill the only guy who could get him home?' asked Jackson.

'I have no idea. It's as big a puzzle to me as it is to you. But it is a mistake and Crolin knows that.'

'Is that helpful to us?' asked Rotsko.

'Oh indeed,' said Ravenhart. 'He will come looking for me. And I may be able to help him. Hunter's don't only hunt, they also set traps.'

Crolin was back in the Sherman Street condo, sitting on the floor in the top room with his back against the wall. In his hand was the Gatetrap. It was decision time and he needed to act. Otherwise things were going to get worse. The killing of the kid was potentially the beginning of a rapid downward spiral, one he needed to avoid. Crolin pressed one button and the green LED came on. He pressed the second and on came the yellow one. Then they settled down to a steady pulse. There, it was done. He took the Gatetrap downstairs and set it on the floor in what would be a lounge. Then he went back upstairs. All he had to do now was wait.

Back at his hotel Ravenhart was sitting in the armchair in his room. It had just gone six thirty. He was reflecting on the day. It had not gone all that well, but Rotsko had rescued it in the end. He was also frustrated at the lack of progress; he really wanted to be on Crolin's tail by now. Then came a faint humming from his small suitcase. It stopped. Then started again.

'So Crolin, the game's beginning.' He got the Gatetrap. The green and yellow fusions were pulsing softly. All he needed to do was activate his own unit and the tracking system between the two of them would be set up. They would be locked into each other. The hunter thought long and hard. The humming had ceased now and the fusions just continued to pulse. He picked up the phone and rang Jackson's cell phone.

'Where are you?'

'Still in the office getting some of the paperwork sorted then I'm off.'

'Could you call around at the hotel on your way. I need you to take care of something for me. I don't want it falling into the wrong hands.'

'Sure, no problem. Be there in about an hour.'

'Thanks.'

Jackson knocked on Ravenhart's door. The room was surprisingly large. Apart from the double bed there was a two-seater sofa and wing chair in front of a coffee table by large ceiling-to-floor windows looking out across the harbour. At this time of night the pier lights were throwing streaks of gold across the satin black water. Some of the moored boats were clearly occupied as they added pools of light to the scene. And across the water the street and house lights of South Portland, where Jackson would be heading shortly, sparkled against the cold black night.

'I'm sorry about earlier today,' said Ravenhart. 'I just felt things were getting derailed and my reaction was out of order. You guys have been very understanding considering what you've had to take on board.'

Jackson was surprised by the apology, but it smoothed the waters between them.

'Not a problem. What can I do for you?'

Ravenhart indicated Jackson to sit in the wing chair and he sat on the sofa. It was then that the detective noticed the strange device besides the hunter.

'I can give a full report of what I'm about to say at tomorrow morning's briefing. The thing is that Crolin has made a move. Come out into the open.'

'Oh! When was this?'

'About an hour ago.'

'You know where he is?'

'Not exactly at the moment, but I will have a good idea later. As I say I can fill everyone in properly tomorrow. The point is, this device,' he tapped the unit, 'is quite important and I really don't want Crolin to get his hands on it.'

Jackson said nothing.

'I need you to take care of it for me tonight and bring it in to the meeting in the morning. If things work out as I think, we will be in a position to trap Crolin before the end of the day.'

'Don't you think we ought to tell Rotsko? And if there's something cracking off tonight shouldn't we have the team on standby?'

'I can brief them in the morning Jackson. There's stuff I have to do tonight and I just need to know that this is in a safe place.' He handed the Gatetrap to Jackson who was surprised at how light it was. A green and yellow LED were pulsing steadily.

'What the hell is this thing anyway? What does it do?'

'Again it will become clear in the morning. For now I just need to activate these.' He reached across and turned a dial. The fusions stopped pulsing, the lights locked on. 'It's a sort of protection mechanism for the device that also helps keep it charged. We're going to need it tomorrow.' He smiled. It wasn't a smile that relaxed Jackson very much. 'Here slip it back in its box and just take care of it.'

'Ok, Ravenhart, I'll do as you ask.' As Jackson got the door he turned and eyed him suspiciously. He felt uneasy. 'You better be levelling with me here.'

Ravenhart patted him on the arm. 'Jackson don't you worry about a thing. We're getting on top of this, believe me.'

Jackson grunted, headed out of the door and

towards the lift. His mood quickly lifted at the thought of the dinner Trish promised him for the evening. He pulled out his cell phone and punched her number.

'I'm on my way. Be there in about fifteen.'

'Ok, Jackson. Take care.'

The humming was back. But this time it was a more urgent and intermittent sound. Crolin leapt to his feet and loped down the stairs. He looked at the LEDs. They were no longer pulsing, but fixed. He flipped open the screen cover. There was the signal, the tracking line and he saw that the hunter was already on the move. Crolin's smile was cruel.

Jackson had spent a long time in the hot shower. Just washing all the tension out of himself. It had been a difficult and not particularly productive day. They had another homicide to the list; Crolin was still loose and now the woman's body found in Riverton three months ago had become part of the case. There was also a side of Ravenhart he'd not seen before. Gone was the relaxed, affable, genial man from Gamlin. Today they had seen the face of the hunter: uncompromising, confident. Not arrogant but with a hard edge. And focussed. The meeting at the hotel still niggled him. His gut told him that Ravenhart was still holding stuff back. Things that they should know. Damn it to hell, things they needed and *should* know. Jackson wondered what had been revealed to Rotsko. Probably not everything.

It was all this boiling around in his mind that had driven him into the shower. Now he sat on the long sofa in Trish's lounge, beer in one hand, a Sade CD sending mellow music into the room. The curtains weren't drawn and he felt himself relaxing as he stared out into the cold, hard, black night. The terrace lights were off and out over the lawns, over the nearby sea, were millions of stars pricking the sky.

He laughed. *And Gamlin wasn't even one of them,* he thought. Jackson didn't know what Trish was cooking, but the smells drifting through from the kitchen made him realise how hungry he was. He'd eaten nothing since breakfast.

'Jackson, do you want wine with this?' she

called from the kitchen.

'That'd be lovely.'

'Well, go into the dining room and sort out what you fancy.'

He got up and walked through, smiling widely to himself. 'I could get used to this,' he murmured.

Just for an instant Crolin wondered if he'd done the smart thing. He was puzzled. The tracking line between him and the hunter should have been getting shorter as Crolin closed in on him. But it had got longer. Both he and the hunter knew they were now locked into each other through the Gatetrap's tracking system. No question about that. They should have been closing in for the final confrontation and Crolin was sure of his plan for coming out on top in that. But now this had thrown him a little. The thought going through his mind which alarmed him was this: *Had the hunter chosen the ground he wanted?*

That wasn't the only problem. Crolin had followed the tracking line. Now he found himself standing in the shadows at the end of Berlin Mills wharf. Large fishing boats were tied up alongside. There were only a couple of security guards about and he'd evaded them without any trouble. But between him and the other end of the tracking line stood the vast, black, swirling expanse of *Fore River*. And he had no idea how to get across.

Reception rang. Ravenhart answered the phone.

'Ryan here Mr Pilkington. Your cab's arrived.'

He gave a curt 'Thanks', replaced the receiver and slipped on his long dark coat. He took one last look around the room. Ravenhart was not planning to be sleeping here tonight — or indeed anywhere near Portland. By the time this night was finished, he planned to be back at the Lodge on Gamlin.

Chapter 10

CROLIN backtracked down the pier and along Commercial Street until he was standing under the flyover that carried the main road to the bridge and across the river to South Portland. He was getting angry. He cut across some wasteland, back to where State Street swept away off York Street and reared up to Casco Bay Bridge. Crolin edged along the sidewalk. Then realised there was a pedestrian way running parallel to the road. He flipped the screen to check the tracking signal. It hadn't moved the other end. Slipping the Gatetrap into his bag, he slung it across his back and set off towards South Portland.

The meal was taken at a leisurely pace. It had been a long time since Jackson had tasted *beef bourguignon*. He'd chosen a *Rioja* to go with it and the couple were sliding away into the night. Trish had ventured a couple of questions about his day, but it was clearly something he didn't want to talk about.

'You ready for apple pie yet Jackson?'

He laughed. 'You're spoiling me m'lady, but let's have a break.'

She got up from the table. 'Come on then.' He took her outstretched hand and they sauntered back into the lounge. They both felt that life seemed perched on the edge of something very special. Trish snuggled up to him on the sofa; they kissed briefly and then talked about what they spent their time doing outside the work environment. It didn't amount to much; both had thrown themselves into their careers for different reasons leaving little room for a social life they didn't really want. They kissed again, this time longer.

'So where do we go from here?' he asked.

'I don't want you to go anywhere Jackson. I want you to stay here. By my side.'

'Thank you Ryan,' said Ravenhart as he dropped his keys on the desk.

Ryan watched Mr Pilkington lope away and wondered why that simple statement sounded like he wasn't coming back. He shrugged, turned and hung the keys on their hook.

Outside Ravenhart climbed into the cab.

'Where to?'

'South Portland.' He'd already found out from Jackson his destination that night.

'It's a big place chief.'

'Head for Cottage Road. I'll tell you more when we get there.'

The driver said nothing. His passenger's brusque manner invited no conversation. He pulled out into Commercial Street, turned up High Street, onto York Street and then swung left and out across the Fore River. Neither driver nor passenger noticed the shape in the shadows of a large man walking across the bridge.

It took Crolin over an hour to find his way through the maze of streets and gardens before he was able to close down the tracking line. He crouched in some shrubs; flipped up the screen. The line had almost merged to a dot. He was practically there. He scrolled the small wheel next to the screen to close further in, looked up and realised the house was not far away. Crolin slid through the trees along Montgomery Terrace and found himself at the end looking down on two houses in Glen Avenue. The tracking line finally merged into a single dot. It was the house on his left.

He skirted round the edge of the trees. A house next to his target had terrace lights switched on throwing a glare across the lawn and up to the edge of a shrubbery. The target house terrace was in pitch black, but soft lights leaked out of the huge picture window. Inside he saw a man and a woman standing together; embracing each other. This was the house, but where was the hunter?

As the cab got towards the end of by Woodbury Street Ravenhart asked him to pull up. 'This will do. I can walk from here.'

'I can take you right to the house you know.'

'That won't be necessary. Here is fine.'

The cab pulled over. Ravenhart paid the driver and got out.

He wound down his window. 'Your change.'

Ravenhart didn't answer. Didn't take the

proffered dollars. He walked away into the night.

'Now that's a strange one,' muttered the driver. He wound up his window, turned round and headed back Downtown. Perplexed.

Crolin moved to the side of the house. He'd tucked the Gatetrap away in the leather bag that was strapped across his back. He certainly wouldn't be needing that now. There was a kitchen window with a smaller one above which was open. Music drifted out. He could hear low talking inside. Crolin sat down leaning against the wall by the back door. That must be the hunter in there. He knows I will come, but doesn't seem to care. It puzzled him. Crolin knew there was a trap. He just had to work out what it was.

Ravenhart was moving fast now through the undergrowth; heading towards Glen Avenue. He knew exactly which house Jackson was in. He'd checked that out when the detective admitted he was going to Trish Longton's place tonight. Information he volunteered when Ravenhart had said he may need to get hold of him quickly. He also sensed Crolin's presence.

Then a voice behind him; 'Excuse me sir.'

'Let's forget the apple pie?' Trish laughed. 'Why Jackson do you have something else in mind?' She put on her best coy face. Jackson laughed; pulled her close; kissed her hard and led her into the bedroom, shutting the door on everything but each other.

Crolin moved round to the picture window. He stood still, faded into the background and watched them. They walked out of view into another room. Crolin moved again. Again he merged into the night and watched as they undressed each other. He was astonished. The hunter naked. No sign of his particle spectrum laser. Crolin wouldn't have a better chance.

Ravenhart turned round. A cop was standing there. His patrol car was across the street with his buddy climbing out of the driving seat.

'Can I help you?'

'Sorry?'

'You appear to be lost. Maybe we can help you get where you're going.' His tone suggested he would like to be of no help at all. It was laced with suspicion. The other cop had joined him at this point.

'No, no. I'm fine. On my way to Glen Avenue.'

'Through the shrubs sir?'

'Look, I mustn't be delayed.'

'If you'd just like to come over to the car sir, so we can check a few things.' He gripped Ravenhart's arm firmly and steered him across the road.

Crolin went to the back door, gently tried the handle. It opened and he stepped inside. He really needed it to be dark. He switched off the kitchen lights, his yellow eyes glowing as he moved through into the lounge. Again he put off the lights and headed towards the bedroom, particle laser in his hand. Aware that he needed only stun the hunter at this point. Crolin stood just outside the bedroom door, the floor making a loud creak under his feet as he pushed it open. The man looked up; shouted something. Crolin realised with horror that it wasn't the hunter.

'Officer I have something very urgent to do now, in Glen Avenue!'

'Just give us a moment sir.' Ravenhart was now getting extremely exasperated. This could go horribly wrong. He had a choice to make. And he had to make it now. 'I have to go.' He made to break away, but wasn't fast enough. The second cop had moved around behind him and cracked him on the back of his neck with his nightstick. Ravenhart crashed to the ground.

'Who the fuck are you?' Jackson shouted. Angry and frightened in equal measure. He flew at the intruder. He heard Trish's sharp intake of breath. Crolin smashed Jackson away with his forearm and ran down the corridor towards the lounge.

'Jackson!' shouted Trish as he leapt to his feet and took after the intruder. 'Jackson don't!' she wailed after him. The man had fled through the back door and Jackson went after him. Fear filled the air.

They lifted Ravenhart to his feet. 'Come on I think we need to take you Downtown.'

'No!' he shouted. 'Ring Brett Rotsko. Now! Tell him you've got Ravenhart!'

The officers looked at each other.

Crolin knew he had got to get away fast. He'd blundered into a trap, but this man was chasing him, shouting at him. Fear began to engulf him. His lips curled.

Jackson stood panting on the terrace looking out into the dark. Trish brought him a robe which he slipped on. 'Come on, he's gone. Let's call the police.'

'I am the police. Go get me a torch.'

He moved onto the lawn. The grass was cold under his feet. He heard something like a snarl away to his left in the shrubs and turned; was shocked to see yellow eyes, glowing, watching him impassively. Jackson moved towards them. Something hit him hard and he saw the yellow eyes over him as he slammed into the ground. Jackson struggled to one knee and then screamed in pain as something lashed around and drove a spike into his back. Trish ran out onto the terrace. Her high pitched scream pierced the night. She saw shrubs shaking as the intruder took flight. Jackson lay on the lawn, feeling his life ebbing away into the frosted grass.

The ambulance had already taken Jackson away by the time McClure arrived on the scene. It seemed absolute chaos. There were a lot of police, dozens of arc lights set up and teams searching through the area. He'd already gone through a police road block set up on Casco Bay Bridge and another one at the top end of Cottage Road with police having sealed off the whole area.

Rotsko came across to him, put an arm around his shoulder and led him towards the house.

'I'm really sorry McClure.'

'What the fuck's actually happened? What was Crolin doing out here?'

'Jackson's not going to survive this McClure.' He ignored the questions. They stopped, colour draining from the Detective Sergeant's face.

'Huh?'

'It's very bad. He was bleeding heavily, from the back. He won't live Sam.'

'Dear God!' They sat on a wooden bench out on the terrace, now lit up like daylight.

'What's happened here chief?'

'Ravenhart set a trap to catch Crolin. It went wrong.'

'Wrong? Wrong? I thought that fucking alien was supposed to be in control! A genius! The great fucking *hunter*!' His explosion of violence ripped through the night; silenced the talking from groups around them. McClure stared at the large patch of blood on the grass. Shook his head. The teams slowly began to murmur around and continued their work.

'So what went wrong?' he asked, subdued.

'Ravenhart was on his way to the house here to catch Crolin. He'd led him into thinking that Jackson was the hunter.'

'Did Jackson know about this?'

'It seems not.' He put a hand on McClure's arm

before he exploded in another expletive-laden tirade. 'Ravenhart did the right thing. If Jackson had known he wouldn't have been able to carry through with the deception.'

'So how did Mr Alien fuck it up?'

'He got stopped by a police patrol.'

'Oh awesome!'

'Not their fault, McClure. Just doing their job. Because Ravenhart couldn't be seen here, he got a cab to drop him off further away. The cab driver was suspicious and reported it. The patrol found Ravenhart heading into the shrubs back up the road and stopped him. He tried to run for it, they stopped him and in that delay, Crolin had struck.'

'Crap!'

'Crap doesn't even begin to cover it.' Rotsko stood up, arched his back. 'They've taken Jackson down to the hospital. Maybe you should go down there.'

'Yeh, I will. He's got no-one else.' Then a thought struck him, 'What was Jackson doing up here?'

'He was with his lady friend.'

'You're kidding me.'

'Nope. She's down at the hospital too. You go. I'm told he doesn't have long Sam. We'll be fine up here.'

McClure headed back to his car, his mind in a whirl. Then he realised that the Assistant Chief of Police had called him by his first name. Things really were serious

Crolin was breathing hard. He'd had to move fast to get away. And he wasn't sure which direction he was headed. So when he hit sand at the edge of water he was momentarily taken aback. It was a black night, but his vision was good. Crolin walked round the bay and came against an outcrop of rocks. He sat down facing out to sea. Behind him the wail of sirens grew in the night. What worried Crolin was that the hunter had laid a trap. He'd walked into it, but the hunter hadn't appeared. He wasn't there to finish off the game. That puzzled him. Hunters didn't make those sorts of mistakes. His first problem though was to get away from the area.

McClure walked into the waiting room. There was a woman there, sitting on the edge of her chair, a pale complexion, her cheeks tear-stained.

'Hi,' said McClure softly,' I'm Detective Sergeant McClure. I work with Jackson.'

'Hello.' Her voice was thin. 'I know, he's told me about you. My name's Trish Longton.'

McClure sat down next to her. 'Has anybody told you anything?'

'Just that they have him in theatre now, but I don't think he's going to make it.' She stifled a sob.

They sat in silence. Several minutes later a consultant came in.

'Hello, I'm Doctor Kirby.' They introduced themselves.

'Is he ...?' Trish couldn't bring herself to say anymore.

'He's still alive, yes. He's a tough one. We've managed to stabilise him, he's had a blood transfusion and we've dealt with the wound in his back ...'

'There's a *but* in there doc.'

'Yes. We have another problem and we're not

sure what it is. He has a high fever, keeps vomiting and fitting. We're waiting for some lab tests.'

'Will he live?' asked McClure.

'I won't lie to you. His situation is critical and unless we can get to the bottom of what's wrong, it doesn't look promising.'

'Rotsko!' It was Ravenhart striding up to him from the bottom of the garden. 'I've found Crolin's trail, but it's gone cold when he crossed the roads.'

'Damn it he can't be far.'

'No, but that's not our immediate problem. It's the initial trail left by Crolin.'

'What do you mean?

'Come with me.' Ravenhart led him into the border. 'It's these.' He flashed a torch at the ground. Rotkso was looking at some sort of animal print on the ground, about twice the size of a man's hand. He looked up at Ravenhart.

'That's Crolin?'

'Yes.'

Rotsko followed the trail through the shrubs. Then the tracks changed into that of a human foot.

'Care to explain what that's about?'

'Not just now.'

'Ravenhart!'

'Not now Rotsko.' His voice was firm. 'First we have to act fast if we're to save Jackson's life.'

'The medics said he had no chance. Said he was losing too much blood from the severe wound in his back.'

'It's not the loss of blood that's the problem; it's the venom.'

'Venom?'

'We need to move. Now!'

Crolin scrambled over the rocks, slipping now and again into the water. It panicked him and he scrambled frantically to get clear. He eventually managed to climb back up to the top and found himself in the grounds of a large house standing on a promontory. The house was in darkness. He skirted round the edge and then started cutting through back gardens, clumps of trees and shrubs; working his way further inland. Crolin could hear search teams moving around. Torch beams sweeping through the night. A couple of times the teams came close. Crolin froze, stood stock still and faded into the scenery.

Two cars, sirens blaring and lights flashing off the surrounding buildings pulled up outside Harbor View Hotel. Ravenhart burst through the doors, strode across to reception. 'Keys. Fast.' He held out his hand. Ryan, open-mouthed, handed them over. Then saw a second man come through the door; tall, grizzled, steel grey hair.

'Sorry to disturb you and the guests,' he said. 'It's an emergency.'

'You the police?'

The man nodded, a faint grin. 'Well, I guess so as those are our cars making all that racket outside.'

A few minutes later Ravenhart emerged from the lift, striding briskly across reception, a small, tan-leather suitcase in his hand.

'See you later, Mr Pilkington,' said Ryan.

'Mr Pilkington?' Rotsko looked quizzically at him.

'Saw it on a car window, Mercedes I think. It's

a company that makes the glass for them.'

Rotsko rang ahead to the Medical Centre and spoke to Dr Kirby; explained that they were coming in with an antidote for Jackson.

It only took them minutes to get there from the hotel. Dr Kirby was waiting for them in a room just outside the operating theatre.

'This is Ravenhart. Best not to ask any questions just now doctor. We can deal with that later. Just listen to what he has to tell you.'

Dr Kirby glanced at Ravenhart then said to Rotsko: 'You need to understand that the patient is in a very critical condition. We're waiting for lab tests to come back. I don't think …'

'We don't have time for this,' interrupted Ravenhart. 'I'm the only one who can do anything for Jackson. Do you understand?'

'Dr Kirby you must listen to …'

The surgeon held up his hand stopping Rotsko in his tracks. 'You have to understand this is my patient. I'm responsible for him. I don't know who this man is you've brought here. If he's a doctor or what. First you at least owe me an explanation.'

Ravenhart ignored him, set his case down on a table and opened it up. It was carefully divided into compartments with numerous objects embedded in the foam-style pockets. Neither Rotsko nor Kirby recognised anything they were looking at. Ravenhart lifted a chrome tube out of one. 'This is similar to the syringes you use. Jackson has been injected with a type of poison. It's not one you have on this planet.'

'Pardon?'

'Leave it for now doctor,' said Rotsko. 'Best you just listen.'

'I'm sorry. This has gone too far,' said Dr Kirby, 'I must ask you to leave. Now.'

Ravenhart carried on. 'This cylinder is already loaded with the antidote you need. There are two chambers inside. One must be discharged into Jackson now and the other one exactly one hour later, is that clear? This is the top.' He flipped back a cap to reveal a small digital screen. 'You press this button to engage, hold the other end against his chest wall over the heart and then push the screen when a violet light comes on. That empties the first chamber and you repeat the process again an hour later.'

'Now, are you going to do this? Because you have virtually no time left to save that man.

The surgeon stared at him, mouth open. He was met by the steady, sure unblinking black eyes. He looked down at the cylinder being held out to him.

'I don't know,' he said to no-one in particular.

The door behind him swung open.

'Dr Kirby you'd better come quick.'

He followed his assistant back into the operating theatre followed by Ravenhart and Rotsko. The scene was one the police chief would never forget.

Jackson was thrashing about wildly on the table; nurses trying to hold him down. He shouted incoherently then vomited a deep green-coloured bile against the far wall. His back arched, he screamed once and then his eyes rolled back into his head. Suddenly everything was still and quiet.

Ravenhart looked at Dr Kirby. 'It's too late. There's nothing I can do now. He's dead.' The man from Gamlin walked out of the theatre, the doors swinging shut softly behind him.

Crolin had finally caught sight of the buildings the other side of Fore River. Downtown Portland was lit up in all its glory. He headed through the large residential area, avoiding discovery. The police road-block was still set up on the entryway to Casco Bay Bridge. He was going to have to bide his time. He came across Mill Creek Park with its large lake, numerous trees and a small outbuilding. Crolin quietly forced the door and went in. It was empty apart from a bench around one side of the curved walls. He lay down, wedging himself against the door and fell asleep.

McClure had nodded off in his office, his head leaning back against the wall behind his chair. Rotsko shook him gently.

'Chief!' He sat up quickly.

'Take it easy Sergeant.'

McClure saw Ravenhart behind him.

'McClure I'm really sorry for what happened out there. Truly. If I hadn't been held up this would have turned out very, very differently.'

McClure was bristling. He wanted to shout at Ravenhart, shake him. Rotsko could see the emotions swarming through him.

'He tried to save Jackson's life, McClure.'

McClure leapt up and kicked the chair across the corridor. 'What the fuck happened out there? How did Jackson die like that? I mean what is Crolin? He's just some guy right? Like you and me chief but from another fucking planet in some fucking place I don't even begin to understand.' He was breathing hard, staring at the far wall. Then he felt as if everything had just been sucked out of him, slumped back into another chair and put his head in his hands.

'God I'm confused. My brain's a mess just now.'

Ravenhart sat down next to him. 'For what it's worth I completely understand McClure. Really. I know this isn't easy for you people.'

'And how would you know that?' There was no malice in the question.

'Well, one day I'll tell you about the first time I

came here. It took me a while to work out how to cross your roads without getting killed.' He chuckled softly. 'And that was the easy part.'

McClure sat back, leaned his head against the wall once again. 'Maybe you'll stay at home next time Mr Alien.'

The day had dawned cold, dark and overcast. Snow was falling steadily and beginning to settle at the roadsides. Mill Creek Park already had a light covering. Crolin surveyed the white expanse from the doorway then set off towards Ocean Street.

At that moment the case team had gathered in Rotsko's office. The atmosphere was subdued. Everyone still in shock about the death of Jackson.

'I know that right now all you can think about is the loss of Jackson,' said Rotsko. 'It's going to take some of you a good while to get to grips with that and I know this next part is hard, but we still have a job to do.' He paused giving time for that to sink in before carrying on.

'We have a very dangerous task ahead of us.

This Crolin kills without question, without feeling. There's no room for people operating at less than one hundred per cent. So if anyone — and I mean anyone — feels they can't give that from here on out just say. I will completely understand.' Rotsko looked around the room before letting his gaze settle on McClure.

The sergeant held his stare. 'I'm not going anywhere chief. I'll be there to help nail that bastard. Jackson wouldn't want it any different.'

Rotsko gave a quick nod.

'Question.' This was Art Williams.

'Go ahead Art.'

'As I understand it, Ravenhart had this antidote with him?'

'Well, at his hotel, yes,' said Rotsko.

'So he knew Crolin had the capability to administer the poison?'

'I did. I know exactly what Crolin is capable of and have prepared for it.'

'So what other tricks has he got up his sleeve?' asked McClure.

'Nothing I can't handle.'

'How did he administer this poison?' asked Art.

'Must have been some sort of knife,' said Rotsko. 'He was stabbed in the back.'

'Not exactly,' said Ravenhart.

They all looked at him. There was a collective sense of wariness in the air. Ravenhart didn't add anything.

'Perhaps you'd care to explain,' said Rotsko.

'Gamlin is about half as big again as the Earth.'

'We don't want a history lesson,' said McClure.

'You're going to need a short one to understand how we deal with Crolin.'

'A large part of our planet has a hostile environment in which few races can live. They've adapted over thousands of years to able to do that. Those don't concern us. That leaves us with two main races. The *Neoferites* of which I am one, we resemble your human race quite closely; the others are the *Arcanates* of which Crolin is one.'

'Well, by all accounts he don't look too dissimilar to us either,' said McClure.

'In one form this is true.'

Chapter 11

With two cops already dead, Portland's Police
Officers were edgy. They really wanted to find who
had done this. It was not that they didn't give their
full attention to homicides, but when their own were
involved it upped the game. So, although the ring
that had been thrown up around a large part of
South Portland last night was no longer in place,
there were more patrol cars than usual in the area.
However, the road block on the downtown side of
the bridge was still there which hadn't pleased those
travelling into work that morning. The two officers
pulled their patrol car into Parkside Terrace and
halted by one of the houses at the end. It was the
only one on the right, backing on to Mill Creek Park.
They knocked on the door. A woman in her late
fifties, early sixties answered.

''Scuse me, ma'am. Sorry to trouble you. We're
just carrying out some checks in the area.'

'Is this to do with that terrible attack up at Glen
Avenue last night? That poor policeman, how is he?

I saw all about it on the TV this morning.'

The two cops looked at each other and ignored the question; 'We just wondered if you heard anything unusual down here last night?'

'No, not at all. It was very quiet.'

'Mind if we take a look round the back?'

'No, carry on.'

The snow had died away to just a few flakes drifting down in the slight breeze. The officers went round to the back lawn and headed through a large number of trees on its far edge, finally emerging in Mill Creek Park. They walked along the edge of the small copse, came upon a summer house. The door was wide open. Tracks in the snow led away to Ocean Street. One officer was already on his radio.

'It may be nothing, but ...'

'Do you mean what I think you mean by; *in one form?*' asked Art.

'Great! We got ourselves a Jekyll and Hyde alien,' exclaimed McClure. Rotsko couldn't help himself and burst out laughing.

Ravenhart was unmoved. Waited for everyone

to settle down. Then smiled. 'I think you'll find it's something a little more disagreeable.'

'So what do we have?' asked Rotsko.

'The Arcanates are what we call *shape-shifters*. You have seen Crolin in his normal form. However certain things can trigger aspects of their physiology. It has happened twice to Crolin in the last couple of days. That indicates a growing level of anxiety, which is good for us. However the fact remains that Crolin has entered a phase where he is both dangerous and vulnerable. And I know exactly how to handle that.'

'Assuming we know where he is,' said Rotsko.

'Of course.'

'So what form does he take?' asked McClure.

Ravenhart stood up and strolled across to the window. Spoke with his back to the room. 'I explained to Rotsko a couple of days ago about the fact that Crolin has been coming back here for 200 years. He has a report for you explaining the details of our chat.'

Rotsko handed folders round to the team. 'I will come to the matter of his other form in a moment.'

Ravenhart turned round. There was little mistaking the determination written in his face. 'Gamlin's interaction with your planet goes back much longer than Crolin's involvement. We, or rather specifically the Arcanates, have a history with your planet going back just over seven thousand years.'

There was an audible gasp around the room.

'Why do you mean them in particular and not yourselves?' asked McClure.

'The Arcanates are unruly. They are not the dominant race, but create problems for us on Gamlin. The Hunters are much like your own police in that they control and deal with unacceptable activity.'

'I think we call it crime,' said McClure.

'Indeed. There are a few Arcanates who have become hunters and they are good. But on the whole they range from being a nuisance to dangerous.'

'So where does Crolin fit into this and why is he here? You also you haven't told us about his other form.'

'I'm coming to that McClure. The fact is that

Crolin's particular line is ancient. It can be traced back to the beginning of Gamlin's involvement here. In the earlier days the Arcanates were just exploring your planet. It went badly wrong very quickly on two occasions. The first involved Crolin's line. Many of them were killed. They've been bent on revenge ever since.'

'Are you telling us that what Crolin's doing here now is revenge for something that happened seven thousand years ago?' asked Rotsko.

'Man, they hold a grudge don't they,' said McClure.

'Where did this take place?' asked Rotsko.

'Here in North America. More particularly in an area which now covers Maine and parts of Canada. The people living here were extremely superstitious and when the Arcanates were seen shape-shifting they were virtually massacred. Of the thirty that came, only seven got away.'

'Weren't they strong enough to overcome an attack?'

'Not when faced with hundreds of them, no,' said Ravenhart. 'Even in shape-shift form.'

'Which is?' asked McClure.

'Well that's tricky. Strong elements of what you'd call reptile,' said Ravenhart, 'but they have a tail like a scorpion. That's how they deliver the venom.'

Less than ten minutes after the cops had made the call, three other patrol cars came into South Portland, sirens going. Already the area was being sealed off and road blocks were up once again on Ocean Street and Cottage Road. The cops were now talking to Lieutenant Austin. 'You did the right thing boys. It may be nothing, but we wouldn't want to take the chance of not doing anything and then regretting it.'

Several minutes later the vans arrived with the dog tracker teams. Snow was falling more heavily once again, virtually covering the tracks which led away from the summer house. The dogs were quickly put to work and picked up a scent leading their handlers away across the park.

'I don't understand why Crolin keeps coming

back after all this time,' said McClure.

'It's burned into their folklore. It's a difficult concept to grasp if you're not an Arcanate, but the fact remains that at a certain point the need for vengeance becomes an almost consuming thing; a call that has to be answered.'

'So they just come back to good old Maine and pick on some poor bastard when it's a full moon or some such thing,' said McClure.

'Oh no. They know exactly who they come to kill.'

It was as if everyone had held their breath. The enormity of Ravenhart's statement weighed heavily in the air.

'You mean Crolin targets someone? He sits in … wherever he lives … on Gamlin, picks a victim and comes here?'

'Victims actually. More or less, yes.'

'Do you know who they are?' asked McClure.

'We have no idea specifically. There is a list of names. We don't know when he plans to come, we only know he's left Gamlin when a specific alarm is triggered on a database.'

'And then they call you,' said Rotsko.

'Then they call the hunters, yes. This is only the second time I've come after him.'

'And he's been doing this for 200 years you say?' said McClure. 'You guys haven't been doing your job.'

'Crolin is probably the most dangerous and accomplished Arcanate in the vengeance field. We've had a lot of success with others.'

'Others? You mean there are more who come here looking to kill our people, 'cos somebody upset them several thousand years ago?' said Blain.

'As I said earlier there were two incidents on this planet that had caused an issue. The other revolves around Egypt and extends back to the time of the Pharaohs. We have dealt with fifteen Arcanates in the time we have been trying to pin down Crolin.'

'He's that good?' asked McClure.

'Believe me, he's better than that good.'

'So what we know so far is Crolin has killed one cop and one youth, both who happened to be in the wrong place at the wrong time, and killed

Jackson because he thought he was you,' said McClure. 'So I take it he hasn't actually properly started yet?'

'That is a puzzle,' said Ravenhart. 'He's been here for just over three months and not struck as he intended. That is completely off-beam for Crolin. He's usually gone again in about that time and probably taken out two or three targets.' He paused. 'Something has gone wrong, badly wrong and I'm not sure what just now.'

At that moment Rotsko's phone rang. 'Excuse me.' He listened. 'Ok let me know if anything further develops.' He put the phone down. 'There's a possible trace on Crolin, but nothing really certain.'

'Where?' asked Ravenhart.

'Over in South Portland.'

'We should get out there,' said McClure.

'Easy,' said Rotsko. 'All we've got at the moment are some tracks in a park. They've got the dogs on them. We've got a bit more to get through here yet. Help yourselves to coffee.'

Chairs scrapped back and the meeting broke up while several of them topped up their mugs. Blain took the opportunity to button Rotsko. 'Chief we still don't know where Sally Johnson fits into all this. Has Ravenhart actually told us anything about Sarmira yet?'

'No, he hasn't. Things have been moving rather fast in the last 24 hours and all the focus has necessarily been on catching Crolin before he kills anyone else.'

'We've had a lot to take on board chief, but we do need to bring Sarmira into the equation now, just like we would on a normal police investigation. We have to see how he fits in and why Crolin killed him.'

'I'm ahead of you Blain. It's firmly on this morning's agenda.'

Howling suddenly filled the air. 'The dogs are on to something.' The two cops ran across the park to where the tracking teams were, just in time to see them disappear up a bank and round the back of some outbuildings on the edge of a small industrial park. Shouts filled the air and as the two patrolmen rounded a corner they saw the handlers unleashing the dogs. A figure cut down a narrow gap between two buildings with a couple of dogs in pursuit. Shouts and barking filled the air. The patrolmen caught up with the handlers.

'We've got him. It's a dead end.'

The case team settled down again and the room went quiet.

'We still have a few things to iron out, Ravenhart, before we plan our next move.'

'I'm sure,' he replied. 'But my main goal is still to get hold of Crolin. This is the closest we've got to him and I don't want this to go wrong now.'

'Your reputation on the line Mr hunter?' McClure was grinning.

Ravenhart gave him a look that chilled him to the bone. 'Sergeant you still haven't fully understood what's going on here. Probably you never will. In your police speak; the guy is a killer and we have to catch him. That's all you need to focus on if the rest is too much for you.'

'Talking of our police way of doing things, there's an issue we need to raise with you, Ravenhart.' Rotsko left a pause. Waiting to make sure everyone tuned in to the next question. 'We want to know how Sarmira fits into this. I don't know if you are aware *how* he died but, as you told me and as we have in the report here,' he tapped the folder in front of him, 'his death, almost certainly at the hands of Crolin, has left Crolin in a position where he is unable to return to Gamlin. You need to tell us what exactly is … sorry *was* … Sarmira?' Rotsko nodded to Blain before Ravenhart had a chance to answer.

Blain went on, 'There's another factor Ravenhart. We have evidence that Sarmira knew a woman who was murdered in August.'

'What evidence is that?'

Blain pushed the photo of Sarmira across the table to Ravenhart. He picked it up. Nodded briefly.

'That is Sarmira. I'm very surprised he allowed himself to be captured in a photo.'

'Given that you say Crolin, and Sarmira, have only been here since the beginning of July and the woman was murdered towards the end of July, that photo must have been snapped between the two events,' said Blain

'It could have been taken at no other time,' said Ravenhart. His mind had gone into overdrive trying to work out what had taken place.

'Who is this woman?' He tapped the photo.

'Her name was Sally Johnson.'

Rotsko didn't think there was anything that could have been said to draw such a violent and explosive reaction from Ravenhart. He leapt to his feet, said one word in a language they didn't understand. McClure guessed, rightly, that it was a Gamlin swear word. Ravenhart's ferocity stunned them all. His black eyes blazing, he swept his hand through his hair and stood there looking at the team, or rather straight through them. His mind elsewhere.

'Ravenhart?' Rotsko broke the spell.

'Sally Johnson was one of the victims on Crolin's list for this visit.'

'How do you know that?' asked McClure.

'You'd be amazed at what we know and how we know it. That's why the hunters are feared on Gamlin if you get on the wrong side of us. We have plenty of experience in tracking and keeping tabs on the Arcanates.'

'You said earlier that Crolin hadn't killed any of his intended victims yet,' said Blain.

'He hasn't.'

'How can you be sure of that?' asked Blain.

'Once we know an Arcanate has left Gamlin on a vengeance mission, bearing in mind by then we have a list of their potential targets, our tracking database tells us when they have struck and how the targets were killed. When Sally Johnson died we know it wasn't done by Crolin. It didn't show up as him on our database.'

'How the fuck does it do that?' asked McClure.

At that point the phone rang. 'Right! We're on our way. Looks like they got Crolin pinned down, if it's him,' said Rotsko. 'Let's go.' Chairs scrapped back, the case team was galvanised. 'We'll come back to this stuff later.'

The dogs were backing out of the alley snarling and barking. 'What the hell's up with them?' said one of the handlers, 'Never seen 'em do that before.' They finally stood their ground, hackles raised. They settled into continuous barking at the dark end of the alley.

'Rotsko's been on the phone,' said Lieutenant Caulk. 'He said to hold off 'til he gets here.'

'Looks like we got no chance, the dogs have backed off. Something down there's spooked 'em bad.' They could already hear the sirens coming across the bridge. Within minutes three cars screeched to a halt in the industrial park followed by an ARV truck. Ravenhart watched a SWAT team disgorge. Dressed in black, putting on helmets with goggles strapped across the front of them. They carried Heckler & Koch MP5s, flash bangs, tear gas grenades and various pistols strapped to their belts. Ravenhart watched them walk past him, not even acknowledging his presence. Walking like they owned the place. A team in black, stark against the snow. They made for Rotsko. The team captain spoke to him.

'Hello. I'm Brady. You in charge here?'

'Yup. I'm the one who put the call in.'

'So what you got down there?'

'Well, we've been after a guy for a couple of days. We think he's holed up down the alley there.'

'You think! You called us in when you weren't sure.' He looked around at the scene and back at Rotsko, clearly unimpressed.

'Captain, the guy we're after has killed three people in the last four days including a detective last night. He's not your regular killer. He is different and extremely dangerous.'

'Let me tell you something bud. I've seen everything man can do to man. I've seen the end results and they ain't pretty. I don't think I'll find anything new here.'

Rotsko pointed at the dogs still standing at the alley entrance; snarling and growling.

'Then they got more sense than you Captain. Because what's down there scares the shit out of them.'

Ravenhart walked over to Rotsko and Brady.

'Can I help here?'

Brady looked him up and down. Taking in the slim build, pale features, black eyes. Watched him sweep his hand through shoulder length black hair.

'Who's he?' he asked Rotsko.

'I'm Ravenhart. You're going to need some info

from me before you send your men down that alley.'
Brady ignored him again.

'What's the name of the guy down there?'

'His name's Crolin. He will kill your men.'

'Mr Ravenhart you just leave this to us, huh?'
Brady walked off.

'That guy's a jerk with an ego the size of
Maine,' said McClure who had come up to see what
was going on.

'He's good McClure,' said Rotsko. 'Trouble is
he doesn't know what he's facing here.'

'Get those fucking wimpy hounds outta here,'
Brady bawled at the handlers.
He stationed four men at the alley entrance. They
crouched down; Hecklers rammed into their
shoulders pointing down into the gloom.

'These men are going to die.' Ravenhart loped
across to Brady. 'You listen to me Captain and listen
well.'

Brady shoved him in the chest to move him
aside, but Ravenhart didn't even sway. The inert
strength took him by surprise.

'Captain, I'm in charge of this operation.' The

ice in Rotsko's voice cut through the tension. 'And don't you forget that. You will move on my orders and not before. Do you copy?'

'Sir, I …'

'Do you copy Captain?'

'Yes, Sir.' He glowered at Ravenhart.

'With all due respect Sir, who the fuck's he?'

'Let's just say he's an expert … no … let me rephrase that; he's the only expert who has a handle on our man down there.'

'Without him Mr SWAT Captain sir, we're all pissing in the wind,' said McClure.

Brady snorted in derision. 'Right so tell me what we got,' he pointedly asked Rotsko.

'His name's Crolin. He has two ways of killing someone and one of evading us altogether,' said Ravenhart.

'And they are?'

Ravenhart looked at Rotsko. 'He's not going to believe us is he?'

'Unlikely. But tell him anyway.'

'Right he can evade you by melding completely into the background. You could be standing next to him and you wouldn't know he was there.'

'Bullshit! What is he, a chameleon?'

'Funny you should mention that.'

'Quiet McClure,' said Rotsko.

Ravenhart ignored the exchange. 'He will kill you by gently grasping your throat here,' he put his hand on Brady's throat just below his Adam's apple, 'and then effectively suck the life out of you. It's quick, quiet and efficient.'

The pause seemed to go on for an eternity as Brady looked from Ravenhart to Rotsko and back again. 'You are fucking crackers. You winding me up, Rotsko?'

Ravenhart still had his hand on Brady's throat. He looked at Rotsko and shrugged. Brady's face gradually flushed. He made a faint gurgling noise in his throat, was unable to make any move of resistance. His eyes started rolling back. Then Ravenhart took his hand away. Brady collapsed to the ground like a sack. Rolled over on his side and then exploded into a coughing fit. McClure struggled not to laugh. Brady sat up and looked at Ravenhart, then Rotsko. He got to his feet and rubbed his throat, but it wasn't sore and he felt no pain.

'I'm sure that helps prove the point,' said Ravenhart. There was nothing in his tone to belittle Brady. But the air of authority in his manner hit the mark.

'I don't understand what just happened there, but I take on board what you've said. How else does this man kill?'

'Boy this is going to be interesting.'

'McClure!'

'Sorry chief.'

'Where I come from Captain, Crolin is what we call a *shape-shifter*. When he makes his transition he is extremely dangerous. Your bullets will bounce of his armoured skin and his scorpion tail moves faster than you can see. The venom is lethal.'

Brady looked at all three of them. Nonplussed.

'And no, I can't demonstrate that,' said Ravenhart, his voice matter-of-fact.   'Crolin and I are from different races.'

Crolin could hear the dogs howling and snarling as he ducked down between the two buildings. They didn't worry him. These weren't going to take him by surprise like last time. He was in control and could deal with them without a problem. They hadn't even chased him into the dark. They were animals and knew what was to be feared and what wasn't. They knew Crolin was something to fear. He realised the alley was a dead end. The walls of the buildings either side were metal and sheer; no fire escape this time. Behind him was a solid concrete wall, about fifteen feet high. Designed to keep intruders out. It also kept Crolin in.

'Can I make a suggestion Sir?' asked Brady.

'Sure,' said Rotsko.

'First we set up arc lights at the top of the alley, then some more halfway down. That should flood the place. It's better than playing games in the dark.'

'Ravenhart?'

He nodded. 'Position your men by the second set of lights, but they mustn't venture further in.' He walked back to the car, got out his small leather case and slapped it down on the roof.

'What's that?' asked Brady.

McClure laughed. 'His box of magic tricks Captain.'

Ravenhart came back with a small object, little bigger than a cell phone but with one end tapering to a fine point.

'And that is?' asked Rotsko.

'It's called a particle spectrum laser. My version of that,' he tapped the Heckler Brady was holding. 'But a little more powerful.'

'Packs a punch, huh?' said Brady.

'You could say that. I won't bore you with too much science, but basically all physical matter is made up of particles, including you and me. This can disrupt them in a manner of speaking.'

Brady raised an eyebrow.

'Depending how I set this, it can do anything from stunning you to turning you into a cloud mass of atoms and molecules. A sort of dust that can't be seen by the eye.' His tight smile left Brady a little unnerved.

'So we see Crolin and *Boom,* off he goes!' said McClure.

'Depends,' said Ravenhart.

243

'On what?'

'If he activates his spectrum shield fast enough.'

Brady laughed. 'Always the same. Someone brings out the ultimate weapon and someone else comes up with the ultimate defence mechanism.'

'Indeed,' said Ravenhart, 'but all the shield does his absorb most of the energy. What gets through will still stun him and then we move in and disable the target.'

'Right, we'd better get the action going.' Brady strode off.

Crolin was waiting to see what they would do. He sensed movement beyond the alley, sensed that the hunter was in the vicinity. His situation was getting dangerous. Suddenly the top end was lit up, bright lights cutting into the gloom towards him. He ran halfway up the alley, melded into the background. Watched. Two teams of two were already moving the next sets further in. A couple of men were so close Crolin could have touched them. He waited as two more joined them. Then he moved

so fast they never had time to register what was
happening.

The screams chilled the blood of everyone.
Brady shouted to four others in the SWAT team and
headed for the entrance, Hecklers at the ready.

'No!' Ravenhart's shout sliced through the air,
but they weren't listening. 'Come back!' There was
no response. The team was locked into its drill for
such a situation. Brady barking orders.

'Stay here,' Ravenhart said to Rotsko. 'All of
you.' He raced across towards the alley. Already
Brady's men had disappeared inside. Seconds later
they were backing out, guns blazing. McClure's
mouth dropped open in horror.

'Oh my fucking God.'

Following them out of the alley was a reptile of
sorts. A deep burgundy coloured beast covered in
tough looking scales. The lizard-like head with
tongue flicking, swayed gently from side to side and,
curved over its back was a scorpion tail with a
vicious black stinger at the end. The whole creature
was about eight feet long. It surveyed its prey with

mesmerising golden yellow eyes.

Ravenhart couldn't get a beam in on Crolin, the SWAT team were in the way. 'Get down!' They continued backing away, firing. Ignoring him.

Crolin shot forward; no-one but Ravenhart registered what was happening. His tale lashed forward piercing one man through the chest, lashed again and caught another in his side. The others ran.

It was at that point that Crolin saw the hunter. In a split second he shape-shifted, moved and melded. A thin, bright-blue beam sliced through the air where he had been, hitting the building. Part of the metal wall buckled. Crolin moved to the back of the alley, shape-shifted again and climbed the end wall; the pads of his feet acting like suckers.

Ravenhart got there just in time to see Crolin's scorpion stinger flicking over the top. He fired at the wall, the beam blowing a hole in it. Ravenhart raced to the gap, but Crolin was nowhere to be seen.

'Maybe you blew him to shit.' It was McClure on his shoulder.

'I told you to stay back,' said Ravenhart.

'Figured you might need a hand. So is he just a

pile of dust out there?'

Ravenhart shook his head. 'It was only on a low setting. I don't want to eradicate him if I can help it. Not unless it becomes absolutely necessary.' McClure looked at the hole in the concrete wall and shook his head.

'I sure wouldn't want to be on the wrong end of that beam.'

'Indeed,' said Ravenhart. Then he patted McClure's arm. 'Thanks for coming in. That took courage when you knew what was going on. I appreciate that McClure.'

'That's ok Mr hunter Alien. Can't let you have all the glory now can we.'

The mood back at the precinct was sombre. Three of the SWAT team had been killed outright, one was in critical condition and two others were also being treated with the venom antidote. Captain Brady and the remnants of his team were in some state of shock as they went through the first debrief. It had been a shambles, no getting away from it. Not only that, their target had escaped. Ravenhart had said little to Brady during the clear up. Brady hadn't listened; hadn't done what he was asked. He reckoned Ravenhart would be more than a little angry. He knew he would be if the boot was on the other foot. Brady also had the problem of trying to come to terms with what he'd just witnessed.

Ravenhart had gone back to his hotel to, in his words, clean up. What he really wanted to do was take time out and think on his own. He also wanted to touch base with the Lodge on Gamlin. Rotsko said the case team needed to reconvene at his office at 2pm, giving them all a break. Time to gather their thoughts. As Ravenhart headed for the lift with his keys, Ryan mumbled that the *old Mr Pilkington was back in town.* Unsmiling, taciturn. Not talkative. He idly wondered what part he was playing in the events in Portland of the last few days. News on the television in his office was reporting now on an incident in South Portland; apparently some gang cornered by police and a SWAT team. People had been killed but officials were saying virtually nothing just now.

Sitting in the wing chair staring out at a grey day with light snow falling steadily, Ravenhart connected to the Lodge Database Chief; Kadine.

'Ravenhart, how's it going out there?'

'Good and bad.' He saw Kadine nod. Ravenhart set the screen on the table in front of him. 'Are we absolutely sure Crolin didn't kill Sally Johnson?'

'Positive. It would have logged on the Arcanate database straight away which we're monitoring through here.

'Sarmira is turning into a big problem, Kadine. Not only should he never have come through the gate with Crolin, he certainly shouldn't have been meeting with one of the vengeance targets. I need some answers and I need them fast.'

'We're working on it Ravenhart. We've got a team going through Sarmira's systems now. Do you think you've any chance of getting Crolin back here?'

'It's getting more difficult. I can't give you any guarantees.'

'If we can get Crolin, of all Arcanates, back here, de-functioned and set up as an example it will be a big, big step forward in our work against the vengeance teams.'

    'I realise that Kadine. As I said I'll do my best.'

    Ravenhart broke the connection and sat back. He was beginning to wonder whether or not the police were becoming a liability for him. Whether once more he should become a lone hunter; consigned to the shadows tracking Crolin.

Chapter 12

IT was 2.30 and Ravenhart still hadn't shown.

'McClure, call his hotel. See if he's left,' said Rotsko.

McClure came off the phone. 'On his way. Left ten minutes ago.' While they were waiting Rotsko gave an update on the injured from the morning.

'Sorry I'm late,' said Ravenhart as he came through the door. 'Been on a call to Gamlin trying to track down some info. I have a question.' He had instantly galvanised the meeting.

'Fire away.'

'Do we have an autopsy report on Sally Johnson?'

'Art?'

'I'll get one mailed through.'

While he was on the phone Rotsko asked Ravenhart why he was after the report.

'The precise cause of death might be helpful to me.'

'To us,' corrected Rotsko.

'Of course.' Ravenhart's smile was brief and not wholly convincing.

'So this morning you were going to tell us where Sarmira fits in. We're kinda anxious to know,' said Blain.

'You are?'

'We are. I don't know how you operate, but we like things nice and tidy.'

'Ok lets then deal with how we get here from Gamlin.'

'Is that necessary?' asked Rotsko

'Well, it's central to Sarmira's activity. But I'll keep it as simple as I can for you. For a start I'll leave out the actual scientific process of how we move around.'

'Fine by me,' said McClure. 'I think spaceship travel is outside my remit.'

Ravenhart laughed. 'I think you'll find it's a little more sophisticated than flying around in a tin can.'

'Especially given the fact we're not just talking about light years away but a parallel universe,' added Webber.

'Thanks for that Bob. Knew I could trust you

forensic boys to drill down to the detail,' said McClure with a thin smile.

'So what are we talking about?' asked Rotsko.

'As I explained before, basically we open what we call a gateway which transports us anywhere off Gamlin. The co-ordinates we use just have to be programmed into the particular database the gatekeepers use. Once a person has been given permission to travel, the gatekeeper is the person they go to see.'

'But you said Crolin wasn't given official permission to come here?' said Blain.

'That's correct. He was banned, as are others, but some gatekeepers are corrupt, others are threatened. The vengeance people have a number of ways of abusing the system however good we are at weeding people out or closing the loopholes.'

'So what about Sarmira?' asked Webber.

'We're going through his systems at the moment to get information which might tell us what's happened down here. As I said before, the disconcerting fact is that if the gatekeeper and traveller get separated neither can get back on their own.'

'How come?' asked Webber.

'You remember the device I asked Jackson to look after?'

'Yes.'

'That is a Gatetrap. When the journey is made it is always held by the gatekeeper. The trap is activated by a key which is in two parts. One is held by the traveller – it's his own personal key designed for him. A second key is held by the gatekeeper. It means one cannot leave the other stranded by returning to Gamlin.'

'*That's* what they are!' shouted McClure.

'Pardon?'

'I'll be back in a minute!' McClure shouted over his shoulder at Rotsko as he shot out of the room.

'So once Sarmira was dead why didn't Crolin just take his key and use both parts on the trap?' asked Webber.

'Because he would have to contact the Gate Lodge to let them know he was returning.'

'And if he was travelling illegally he couldn't have done that,' said Blain'

'Precisely,' said Ravenhart, 'It is the gatekeeper's job to make contact, which is why I can't understand why he killed Sarmira. He was his only ticket home. Apart from me.'

At that point McClure crashed through the door. He put two plastic bags on the table in front of Ravenhart.

'I'm guessing these are the keys,' said McClure.

'Indeed.' He raised his eyebrows. 'Where did you get them?'

He pointed to the round one. 'This one I came across halfway up a fire escape in the alleyway where we found Sarmira's body. The history of the other one is more interesting.' He explained about the hidden photos found at Sally Johnson's remote house outside Caribou and that the rectangular-shaped key was found in the envelope with them.

Ravenhart frowned. 'The round one is Crolin's, but he must have lost that after the killing. The other is Sarmira's. The gatekeepers always have that one. But why Sally Johnson had that is an absolute mystery to me just now.'

'You said; *apart from me,*' said Blain.

'Sorry?'

'When talking about Crolin not being able to get back with Sarmira being dead.'

'Oh, yes. Because of our work, hunters have different travel arrangements.'

'Club class seats I guess,' said McClure.

'We don't use gatekeepers. We have our own Gatetrap. It works differently and only needs one key. We activate it and go straight back to the Hunter's Lodge. If Crolin got hold of my Gatetrap he could get back to Gamlin.'

'Forgive me,' said Webber, 'but with all your sophistication that seems rather lax security.'

'And wouldn't it also dump him straight into the arms of your people?' added Blain.

'Nothing's foolproof in these universes and the technology of gatekeeper travel makes the traps necessarily flexible. And no he wouldn't go back to the Lodge. The hunter can set his own co-ordinates. So could Crolin.'

'Is that why you set the trap with Jackson? Because you knew Crolin would home in on your device that Jackson was holding?' asked Blain. Ravenhart nodded.

South Portland was completely locked down. Road blocks were set up on all main routes out. There were blocks on both ends of the bridge and armed police guarding the pedestrian route across to downtown Portland. There had been no sign of Crolin which puzzled the search squads but not Ravenhart and the case team. Once sure the area where he'd vanished wasn't being watched, Crolin re-emerged and headed away to another industrial park off Waterman Drive. He realised there were only two ways back across the bay: over the road bridge or swim. And swimming was definitely out of the question. Arcanates couldn't deal with water: he'd drown. Crolin also realised that this time he wasn't going to be able to just walk across the bridge.

In a car park used by several units Crolin found what he was looking for: a truck by the loading bay of a small warehouse. Cardboard boxes were being piled inside. He moved towards it; stopped as a man

carrying a box came out of the nearby building.
Crolin merged into the background. As soon as the
man went back into the building Crolin climbed into
the truck, shifted a couple of boxes forward and
crouched down behind them. It was about another
30 minutes before he heard someone get in the cab,
slam the door and fire up the engine. Several
minutes later he felt a jolt as the truck lurched
forward and moved out. They hadn't been going long
when it pulled up and the engine switched off. Crolin
wondered what was going on.

The road block on the road leading up to the
bridge was set up as a double chicane. It was part
way across the lane leading to downtown Portland. A
little further back across the rest of the lane was a
further set of blocks. There was no chance of
anyone racing through. They had to slow right down
to negotiate their way through. On front of that was a
barrier, this time right across the road. Behind it were
four cops armed with Hecklers and in front three
others pulling up the traffic. As the long wheelbase
Chevrolet Express van approached, one of the cops
held up his hand. The van stopped.

'Kill your engine bud.'

'This about that shoot up earlier this morning?'

The cop ignored him. 'Where you off to?'

'Up state to Presque Isle. Delivering stationary stuff. Just hoping this snow ain't going to get worse, otherwise the trip'll be a nightmare.'

'That's for sure. Did you load up the truck?'

'Yup.'

'When?'

'Finished about forty minutes ago.'

'How long did it take ya?'

'I'd say 45 minutes tops. Why's that?'

'Never mind. We're going to have to take a look inside. Sorry bud.'

The driver climbed out, went to the rear of the van, unlocked and swung open the rear doors. The cop stood on the bumper and flashed his light inside. The boxes weren't quite to roof height, but it was tightly packed.

'You're going to need to shift some of that out.'

'Hell man I'm late away already! Do we have to? It's going to take me five hours as it is and it's nearly three already.'

'Quicker you do it, quicker you'll be on the road.'

The driver started lifting the boxes out on to the road. After about fifteen minutes he'd emptied half the van. The cop climbed inside and shone his torch over the rest.

'Hey bud how come there's a gap near the back there? You sloppy at packing or what?'

The driver climbed and took a look.

'Beats me. I'm sure I packed 'em in tight. But they're all here anyhow. Can I load and go?'

'Yup, do it. Have a good trip to Presque Isle bud. Hope the weather's kind for you.'

As the doors shut and the back of the van was plunged into dark, Crolin stretched himself as much as he was able in the confined space. He couldn't believe his good fortune. The truck was zeroing in on where he needed to be.

On Gamlin, Kadine took a call. 'We have stripped the data out of Sarmira's system. I'll flash it across to you at the Lodge.' It was Langard, head of the security unit.

'Thank you,' said Kadine. 'You boys taking a look at it now as well?'

'Yup we're running it through the bank to shake out the irrelevant stuff. I'll call you when we're done.'

Within seconds the data had dropped into Kadine's terminal. He opened it up and started reading. After ten minutes he'd come across nothing unusual. Everything seemed to be in place. Just as he and Ravenhart had planned it out. He put the call in.

Ravenhart's cellpack hummed. He took it out of his pocket; the violet fusion was pulsing. 'Excuse me.'

He left the room. 'Kadine. Any news?'

'We've stripped the information out and the team is working on it at the moment, but I'm checking through stuff here as well. I can't see anything that shows why Sarmira should have killed Sally Johnson. It was never part of our plan, Ravenhart and I don't see why Sarmira would veer away from that.'

Ravenhart then went on to tell him about Sarmira's key being found at the woman's house.

'There's something very wrong here Ravenhart. Very wrong.'

Back in Rotsko's office Ravenhart took his seat. He was pensive. Art Williams was talking, giving a rundown of the autopsy report on Sally Johnson.

'There's no obvious cause of death,' he waved the report. 'It's just like she stopped breathing. To put it in medical terms: *an abrupt failure of ventilation occurring through respiratory acidosis.*'

'I'm assuming your report has a question mark over the surprising lack of blood carbon dioxide considering this apparent cause of death.'

Art looked back at the report. 'It does.'

'Remember the demonstration I gave Brady this morning showing one of the two ways that Crolin could kill? Well, what you have there in your report is the consequence of that method of killing. You'll find the same thing in Officer Logan's autopsy report. But Crolin didn't kill the woman.'

'Who did?' asked Blain.

'Only two other people could have done that,

either me or Sarmira. And it wasn't me.'

Rotsko started asking Art more questions about the report. Webber and McClure were talking to each other. Ravenhart was quiet again. Distracted. He had to come to a decision and quickly. Otherwise Crolin would kill his next victim. And Ravenhart knew exactly who that would be.

Chapter 13

THE light on Kadine's small screen was flashing. He passed his hand over it and Langard's face appeared. He looked worried.

'We have a major problem, Kadine.'

'Go on.'

'At best it looks like Sarmira's cover was blown. If that's the case, Ravenhart is in extreme danger.'

'Why's that?'

'Because an encryption code in agent Sarmira's database has been set off.'

'Meaning what?'

'It has almost certainly triggered an alarm with the Arcanate security.'

'How has that happened Langard? They're not apparently that advanced.'

'We had suspected they were, but weren't sure. Now we are.'

'So why is Ravenhart in danger?'

'Crolin is the pivotal figure of their vengeance

programme. They may well break with their protocol and send a team in to pull him out. It will mean the death of Ravenhart in the process.'

'What do I tell him? He's one of our top two hunters. I can't afford to lose him.'

'Tell him nothing at the moment Kadine. You may have to sacrifice him.'

Langard closed the link. Kadine stared at the blank screen. Grim faced.

Ravenhart had come to a decision. 'Rotsko I need to talk to you. In private.'

'If it's to do with the case, then the team needs to be in on this,' said Rotsko.

'No, they don't Rotsko. There's nothing this team can do anymore. We don't need it. It's not going to be helpful.'

'That's not your decision.'

Ravenhart leant forward. 'It's not up for discussion.'

Rotsko didn't respond.

'You just want to trash us now, is that it?' said Blain.

'I can make any decision I want to Rotsko. But we need to talk.'

He gave a curt nod. 'Ok we'll break up here.' He looked at his watch. It was almost six. Outside the snow was falling steadily, but it was still light. 'Everyone go get something to eat. I want you back here in an hour.'

The white Chevrolet van pulled off *Route 95* north of Bangor and on to Kelly Road, turned right on to Main Street and headed towards Orono. The main route had been cleared of snow but as the van travelled further north where the snow was starting to become thicker it was now swishing through slush. After a couple of miles it pulled off into a diner car park on the outskirts of the town. The driver was hungry. The diner was called *Barney's Cruisin Diner*. The name was lit up in red across the double fronted building. There were only a few cars and trucks in the park and the diner windows were steamed up. With the weather closing down, there weren't going to be many people on the road for much longer, thought the driver.

He sat in a cubicle. A waitress, trying to look in her twenties but going on forty, came over, pad at the ready.

'What can I getcha?' She pulled a pencil out from behind her ear. Mousy brown hair was fighting to stay under her cap.

'Fish chowder, big bowl of salad, plate of fries and a shake.'

'Flavour?'

'Make it double choc.'

'K.' She walked off.

He looked at his watch. It was at least another two hours to Presque Isle. The television mounted on a wall across from where he sat was giving out a weather report. Snow most of the night, travelling conditions very tricky off the main routes later that night and into the early hours. Higher temperatures in the morning would see off most of the overnight snow. He was going to have to stay over. He rang the office back in South Portland. With a 24 hour delivery service, there was always someone on duty. He told the girl to book him an overnight room in Presque Isle and let him know. Thirty minutes later he left the diner. He was alarmed to see one of his back doors opened. He ran across, sliding on the snow as he went and looked inside, breathing heavily. 'I'm sure I shut that properly.' He shrugged as he shut the door, making sure the latch caught, and was surprised to see footprints other than his own at the back of the van. They led away in the snow, stopped and came back again. He opened the back doors and checked everything was fine. 'Weird.' He got in the cab, fired up the engine, pulled out onto the road and headed back to *Route 95*.

Inside, Crolin settled down once again to another cramped few hours, but glad he'd had the opportunity to get out for a good stretch.

After they had all filed out, Rotsko shut his door. He sat behind his desk. Ravenhart sat opposite him.

'So what's this about?'

'I've not told you everything.'

'You've not told me everything.'

'No. It wasn't necessary. You needed to capture Crolin, so did we. I told you as much as you needed to know to reach that goal.' Ravenhart's blunt but honest approach took any sting out of the anger that had been rising in Rotsko.

'Are you going to enlighten me?'

'Sarmira was working for us.'

'Us being?'

'The hunters.'

'So he wasn't a gatekeeper.'

'Oh yes, he's always been a gatekeeper. We recruited him as an agent to set up Crolin.'

'Right.'

'Sally Johnson was working for us as well.'

'What?'

'Well, with us.'

'You'd better tell me what this is all about Ravenhart.'

'At one time the Arcanates were a nuisance, but we could keep them under as much control as necessary. In recent times, which is about 200 years as far as we're concerned, they have begun to become a direct threat to the balance of power on Gamlin. The Arcanates were once tribal and disparate. Now they are becoming cohesive and focussed.'

'What's changed to cause that?'

'The vengeance teams. They have, and still are, growing in status as the folk lore surrounding them has become better known. They are beginning to be held up as the strong face of the Arcanates. The deeds of the vengeance teams are encouraging them to believe they have the power to bring about change and authority for the Arcanates on Gamlin. An authority they don't have at the moment.'

'Let me guess. Crolin is critical to this.'

'As you say. He is not only a strong voice, but is a formidable seeker of revenge. His exploits are the stuff of legends among the Arcanates. He is on the brink of being the person to lead a revolution on Gamlin. A revolution that would be destructive for all but the Arcanates.'

'So you need to kill him.'

'Absolutely not. Then he'd just become a martyr. We need to dysfunction him so that the Arcanates understand their place in the law and order of things on Gamlin.'

'So why no team?'

'I didn't say *no* team, I said *not that* team. I know where the end game is going to take place and I need a team capable of doing this right.'

'So how and why did you recruit Sally Johnson?'

'Because of the way we were setting the trap I needed Sarmira and Crolin in the same place. So we could take Crolin out and get him back to Gamlin. To do that we had to let her in on what was going on.'

'How did she take that?'

'Surprisingly well.'

'There is an anomaly in all this though isn't there?' Rotsko was astute as ever.

'Go on.'

If Sarmira and Sally Johnson were working for you, why did he kill her?'

'That's what worries me.' Ravenhart frowned.

'So how do you want to play this from here on out?'

'We're going to have to head north.'

'North!'

'Yes, it's where Crolin will be going.'

'It's unlikely he's even got out of South

Portland, never mind going north,' said Rotsko.

Ravenhart gave him a look.

'He's gone?'

'No doubt about it Brett. He has the skills to avoid anything you can set up.'

'Shall I stand the road blocks down?'

'That's your call.'

Rotsko looked out the window, deep in thought. He knew he'd never really been in full control of the operation to date. That Ravenhart had been driving it from the background. And he'd always suspected there was more than Ravenhart was telling. But now he felt that the full deck was finally on the table. There were questions that neither he nor the hunter from Gamlin had answers to just yet, but Ravenhart said they had to go north. Well, they might as well do that because Rotsko didn't have an alternative plan. Now he just wanted Crolin off the planet. He could deal with the mopping up here.

'Ok, we'll play it your way. So why change the team?'

'Webber and Williams are going to be of no

use to us now. Neither is Blain because with Jackson dead he's going to be your lead detective in Portland. He'd be more use here.'

That made sense to Rotsko. 'What about Carson and Loey they've been pretty much kicking their heels.'

'I will need them along with Brady and two of his SWAT team.'

'Brady? Don't you think he stepped out of line when we had Crolin cornered?'

'You told me he was a good SWAT team leader right?'

'Yup.'

'Well, that hasn't changed. At least he now knows what he's dealing with.'

'True. And I assume me and McClure are in on this.'

'Indeed.'

Rotsko looked at his watch. 'The others will be waiting outside. Let's get them in and you can let them know who's on the team and who's out.'

It was all done in 30 minutes. The only one who clearly wasn't happy was Webber, the other two accepted the decision without too much problem. The new team was to meet up at 6.30 the next morning and after they'd all gone Rotsko put a call into Brady.

It was almost 9pm and the driver still hadn't got into Presque Isle. The trip up *Route 95* had got more difficult in the snow. Less traffic on the route meant more snow settling. Near Houlton, not far from the New Brunswick border, he had to turn left onto *Route 1* which took him up to Presque Isle and driving conditions became even more hazardous. By the time he reached the town, staff at the warehouse had long given up waiting for him so he made straight for the motel on Pond Street. He parked up, locked the van and headed indoors.

Crolin waited a good 30 minutes before making any move. It took him several minutes to shuffle the boxes about so he could get to the rear doors. He jumped out. He was greeted by a white landscape. The temperature was also dropping. Neither bothered him. He was only about fifteen miles from his next target. Crolin would be there by morning and, once the killing was complete, he could focus on getting back to Gamlin. Already a plan was in place to reach that goal.

He set off. The weather was to his advantage. There was nobody else out on the streets. He took the State Street bridge across the river, headed up Main Street, onto North Street and made for Fort Road which would lead him out of Presque Isle and towards border country. He moved at a brisk pace, the snow forming a mantle on the shoulders of his coat. Crolin had little doubt about the success of this vengeance killing. It was vital. Publicly humiliating both the hunters and the Neferites would be dynamite for the Arcanates. It would also once again please his ancestors. The on-going revenge for a massacre that took place 7,000 years ago. The vengeance killings that would never end.

It was still dark. Snow lay on the ground, but already downtown Portland was coming to life for another day. The cab dropped Ravenhart off at the precinct. Rotsko was already in his office even though it was only 6am.

'An early starter as well eh, Ravenhart?'

'Yes. What are the conditions like up north?'

'They had more snow than expected last night, but the main routes have been cleared. So where are we heading?'

'Caribou to start with. Where we go after that depends on several things, but it won't be far.'

'Do you think Crolin's got a start on us?'

'Undoubtedly, but he's going to have a frustrating morning while we're on the road.' He smiled.

'Who's the target?'

'I'd rather not say just yet.'

'Ok, that's fine.'

When the rest of the team had arrived Ravenhart gave them a run down on the situation, leaving out much of what he'd told Rotsko. It wasn't necessary for the operation they had to complete.

'Crolin's headed north. We know where he's going and who he's after. We are going to lay a trap for him and it's vital you do as I say. If anyone steps outside the plan it will probably be fatal for all of us.' Ravenhart looked at Brady.

He nodded. 'Not a problem there.'

'Good. We're leaving in ten minutes.' Chairs scrapped back. 'There is one other thing.'

Everyone one stopped. Ravenhart made sure he had their attention.

'Rotsko has agreed to this. There is only one goal for this operation. Crolin will be taken alive and taken back to Gamlin.'

'You can't be serious!' exploded McClure. 'The guy's a cop killer. He's killed other people. He needs to be dealt with here. And another thing, how the hell would we square it with the authorities and the press?'

'Ravenhart has provided me with certain information that means Crolin has to be taken back to Gamlin, alive. Trust me there is more at stake than you can begin to imagine. As far as the fall-out is concerned we can deal with that McClure.'

'Like how chief?'

'Like the killer is trapped up country. He's dangerous. SWAT team called in. There's a shoot out ... you want me to lay it all out for you.'

McClure shook his head.

'That's also why nothing must ever … *ever* … be said outside this team about today's events or anything from the previous few days involving Crolin. It will all be buttoned down. There'll be nothing on file. You all got that?' There were murmurs of ascent. 'Good. Let's go.'

Fort Fairfield is never going to bask in the spotlight. The town in Aroostook County has a population of less than 4,000 and nudges the New Brunswick border. The main business is agriculture — potatoes and broccoli to be precise. The spring surge on the *Aroostook River* can be a problem but the levees usually cope with that. Now though, life begins to get harsh in Fort Fairfield. It has 96 inches of a snow a year compared to the Maine State average of 73 inches and the 25 inches average for the whole of America.

First light revealed that there was already a good covering of snow in and around the small town. Most of the township was sprawled along the south side of the *Aroostook*. The place Crolin was looking for was on the north side. There was only one bridge over the river and Crolin was well aware that he was the only person on foot. Anyone else out and about were inevitably driving four-wheel drive pick-ups and trucks. He walked along Limestone Road heading for the bridge. Hunkered down in his coat as if trying to hide from view. The cold certainly didn't bother him.

Officer Taplow was sitting in his car in Pool Drive. The heater on. His partner had gone to the cafe across the street to get them a couple of hot drinks. A man on foot came into view. He walked past the front of the patrol car.

'You're a big fella,' said Taplow to himself. He watched him walk up the road. The passenger door flung open and McCausland clambered in, handing a mug of coffee to Taplow.

'Did you see that guy?' said McCausland.

'Yeh, probably some hobo.'

'Not one I've seen before. But why's he heading north. If he's going anywhere it should be south away from this shit.'

'Ah leave him be,' said Taplow.

'No, I'm curious. Come on lets go.' They put the coffees in the drinks holders and Taplow eased the car out on to Limestone Road. The man was nowhere to be seen. There was nowhere for him to disappear to. No alley to duck down. That part of the road just led straight to the bridge.

'Huh? Where'd he go?' said Taplow. 'Pull over here.'

McCausland stepped out of the patrol car. In the snow were one set of footprints on the sidewalk which suddenly stopped.

'What the …?'

They looked at each other. Crolin watched them.

The team had packed themselves into an ARV. It wasn't that comfortable, but it would get them through the snow and carried everything they needed. They were two hours into the journey up *Route 95* when Ravenhart's cellpack hummed. It was Kadine.

'I'll call you back.' He didn't want to be having this conversation with everyone listening in.

'Girl back home?' asked McClure.

The others laughed.

'Nope. My chief. Can we pull over some place?'

'Sure,' said Brady. 'We got a road diner about eight miles on. Will that do you?'

'It'll do,' said Carson. 'I need something to eat.'

'That will be fine,' said Ravenhart.

What the others hadn't heard was Kadine's comment; 'Ravenhart, we have a major setback. Can you talk?'

For the next eight miles Ravenhart was sunk deep in thought, trying to work out just what had happened back on Gamlin. The truck pulled into the diner park and disgorged the team. They stretched, stamped their feet, chatted and headed to the warmth of the diner.

'Can I get you anything?' Rotsko asked Ravenhart.

'Mug of tea will be fine. I won't be long.' He watched them go in, pulled out his cellpack and called Kadine. He climbed back into the truck. The screen flashed on and Kadine appeared looking tight-faced. A worried crease across his forehead.

'What's happened?'

'We got the data scan back from Sarmira's system. Our mission has been compromised.'

'Since when?'

'Since the start. They'd got to him. The Arcanates.'

'Go on.'

'They'd turned him, Ravenhart. He was a double agent from the day he and Crolin left Gamlin. He was never going to let us get to Crolin, he was never going to prevent the vengeance killings.'

Ravenhart's brain was racing trying to work out the implications.

'But why did he kill Johnson? He knew we'd be on to that and discredit any claim Crolin made.'

'We're not sure and it actually makes Crolin's killing of Sarmira a double mystery. The data so far shows us that an Arcanate subterfuge team had been working with Sarmira some months before he left. He never actually met with Crolin until the day of departure, but had been fully briefed about the operation, about frustrating our plans, about dispatching the target and getting back to Gamlin.'

'How the hell did we not become aware of that?'

'They played it well. There's something else as well.'

'What?'

'They obviously didn't know who was assigned to the case. As usual we kept that aspect strictly between the hunter lead team and the hunter. However, regardless of that, their plan was also to take out the hunter. That was a *must* to score a major propaganda coup.'

'They must be confident.'

'Well, with us unaware of Sarmira's position it would have put them in a strong position to do that.'

'So where do you think all this sits now, Kadine?'

'I think Crolin still plans to take out the second target and I think with the loss of Sarmira, killing you becomes a major goal for them now.'

'That's certainly going to make things interesting. But Crolin's on his own now. It's not going to be so straightforward for him.'

'Just take care Ravenhart.'

'Oh, I always do.'

'The data team are drilling down deeper into Sarmira's systems to see what else they can come up with. I'll keep you informed.'

The picture faded. Ravenhart was lost in thought, his breath spiralling away in the cold when the diner door crashed open and McClure yelled for him to come inside. He grabbed the mug McClure was holding for him and went in. 'Thanks. Go grab Rotsko and come down here.' Ravenhart made for a cubicle away from the rest of the team. He told them about the call from Kadine and filled in some of the gaps for McClure.

'What does that mean for us?'

'On the surface, no change,' said Ravenhart. 'Crolin's still on his own as he was before the call, so the plans and goals don't change. Kadine will let me know if anything else comes up otherwise we just go ahead as planned.'

'So all this political-type stuff is why you need Crolin back on Gamlin in your care?' said McClure.

'Precisely.'

'Time to move out,' said Brady. He waited for everyone to leave. 'You ok?' he asked Ravenhart in a low voice as he passed.

'Sure, Brady. Nothing's changed, just some back information we can deal with later. Thanks.'

A few minutes later the ARV was back on *Route 95* heading north.

As soon as he had crossed the bridge, Crolin dropped off the highway and followed the river, parallel with North Caribou Road. He was in the tree line which meant snow was lighter on the ground and the going a little easier. Crolin kept ducking out and checking his whereabouts. Eventually he saw the house just up a slight hill from the water's edge. It was on its own. A yellow-cream double-fronted place. There was a porch at the back of the house. In the summer it was a good place to sit, catching the sun for most of the day. In the centre were a set of double doors and windows either side. There were also two windows in the roof. To one side was a garage and next to that a large wood shed with plenty of timber stocked up for the months ahead.

Crolin crouched down next to a tree and watched. Waiting to catch some sign of life. Waiting for the target to show.

After four hours the team rolled into Presque Isle. It was close to noon and Brady had suggested that it might be wise to get something to eat before going any further. Ravenhart agreed.

'We're only about twelve miles from our destination,' he said. 'I'll need to give you the final briefing, but we need somewhere out of the way. I don't want it looking like some gun show has rolled into the town.'

Rotsko put a call into Caribou police department and spoke to Jav Wilcox, the chief of police. They had already been briefed by Portland about the operation on their patch who had said, 'Thanks but no, we don't need help on the ground. It was a State incident.'

'You guys in town already?' asked Jav.

'Not yet, but we'll be there in about twenty. We need to be discreet and we need a briefing place.'

'No worries. Just pull up in our parking lot at

the side and you can bring your team in through the back.'

Thirty minutes later they were in a large, wood-panelled meeting room in Caribou Police precinct on High Street. Coffee, sandwiches and donuts had been laid on for them. Jav had said, 'Hi' to everyone and left them to it.

'I just want to make it clear that this is Ravenhart's show from here on in people,' said Rotsko. He sat back and nodded at the Gamlin hunter.

'Our hunting ground is on the outskirts of Fort Fairfield. A house on its own off North Caribou Road. We'll get maps up on the screen in a minute. Crolin should already be in the vicinity. It's the home of his target, Rebecca Johnson.'

'Johnson?' said McClure.

'Yes, the daughter of Sally Johnson.'

'He was planning to kill both?'

'Indeed they are part of the same family line that Crolin has been targeting for years, as have others before him. Unlucky for Crolin she's not there just now, somebody else is.'

'How'd that work?' asked Brady.

'I got in touch with Jav Wilcox yesterday and asked him to move the daughter out and leave a decoy behind. We wanted the house to look lived in.'

'So how are we going to play this?' said Brady.

Ravenhart's cellpack hummed. 'Sorry I'm going to have to take this.' He passed his hand across the screen and Kadine's face came up.

'Neat,' said McClure as Ravenhart moved away to the door and out into the corridor.

'Sarmira panicked!'

'What?'

'They've traced contacts on his system. He killed Sally Johnson by accident. There was some sort of confrontation concerning his gatetrap key which she was holding on to. He'd been in touch with the Arcanate subterfuge team to let them know what happened. From other information we've since picked up it seems that Crolin then lost it with Sarmira when he realised he'd been deprived of his honour killing. I'm guessing the argument was more violent than intended.'

'How'd you get hold of that?'

'People we've had on the inside for some time, that's all you need to know. We've pulled them out this morning. Things are getting tight there.'

'Right but nothing for us here now. We can deal with that sort of stuff when I get back.'

Kadine said nothing.

'What else?'

'A gatekeeper and Arcanate left Gamlin this morning. They're both members of the subterfuge team. They're coming for Crolin.' He paused. 'And you.'

Chapter 14

CROLIN saw someone appear in the left hand window at the back. Just a shape, but it was enough. It was time to go in. Then a movement caught his eye away to the right. Someone or something moving in the trees along the river edge. Crolin froze, melded into the scenery and waited. He saw movement again. Definitely somebody down there. And they weren't out for a walk in the snow. They were stalking.

Ravenhart walked back into the room. His face stern, his eyes hard. There was a wariness about him that Rotsko hadn't seen before.

'Everything ok?' he asked.

'Not exactly. We may have company.'

'Company? What sort of company?' asked McClure.

'The sort of company that has just made our work a little more difficult.' A house flashed up on the screen. It stood on its own. No trees or shrubs. Open

ground all around it.   'This is the Johnson place.
The nearest cover is a line of trees down by the
river.'

'So it's an open ground operation,' said Brady.

'Yup. I want one of your SWAT men down by
the river. He can cover the area from there. Brady I
want you with me and McClure inside the house.
Rotsko I want you Carson, Loey and the other SWAT
operative here in the wood shed.'

'If Crolin's already there, won't he see us all
piling in? And, if he goes all chameleon on us we
won't see him,' said McClure.

'The first part won't be a problem,' said
Ravenhart.

'Let me guess; some more Gamlin fancy
wizardry?'

'The second part will only be a problem if
Crolin never moves and I'm thinking he'll be doing a
bit of that.'

'How do you mean?'

'He only stays melded into the background if
he doesn't move. Once he takes a step, the cover
breaks.'

'What's the company, Ravenhart?' asked Brady.

'Two more Arcanates were detected leaving Gamlin this morning. It's safe to assume they're on their way here. Apart from rescuing Crolin they have also been told to kill me.' It was a straight statement from the hunter. No emotion, just another fact delivered to the team.

'Fuck that,' said McClure.

'I appreciate your support.' Ravenhart smiled at the Detective Sergeant.
'Once we get into Fort Fairfield we will park up on the south side of the river. After that I can get us into place without any problems.'

'How do you want us to actually handle the confrontation?' asked Brady.

'The key is going to stop Crolin shape-shifting. If he does that we'll have one big problem on our hands. If we stun him I can move in and neutralise him with the particle spectrum. The job's done at that point.'

'And if the *company* join in?' asked Rotsko

'Call in the cavalry,' said McClure.

'As you say. Rotsko and the rest can surprise them from behind. Once Crolin's down we can take the others out of the equation. Completely.'

Crolin moved carefully back down to the tree line, merged into the background again and waited. The figure was now away to his left; looking up at the house. He sensed there was someone else nearby. He didn't move. A woman came out onto the porch of the house and was sweeping snow off the steps. Crolin was annoyed. That would have been a perfect moment to strike. He looked back at the figure and saw another standing there now. Crolin crept up behind them. In a split second he felled one with a blow to the back of the neck and kicked the backs of the knees of the second so he crumpled to the ground.

'You still have some learning to do.' His voice was gruff.

The two Arcanates stood up. Harrigan rubbed the back of his neck, Brynchek swore.

'Don't they think I can manage a woman on my own?'

'They want the hunter taken out,' said Harrigan

'Who is it?'

'Ravenhart.'

Crolin was silent for a moment. 'He's one of their best.'

'Exactly. Taking him out will be a major coup for us. And they want us to be sure the job is done.'

'So I'll kill the woman, then we need to get back to the city and set a trap for Ravenhart.'

'There's no need,' said Brynchek. 'He knows you're here. So he will be here too.'

'How does he know I'm here? In this place?'

'Sarmira told them who was on your vengeance list. He'll be here.'

Crolin was unnerved by that piece of information. Any hunter holding those cards would be a problem. Ravenhart holding them could only mean serious trouble. No matter how many were helping Crolin.

The team were back in the truck and heading out of Caribou. Everyone was quiet, thinking through what lay ahead, or at least trying to work out what might happen. There were too many unknown equations to plan everything down to the last detail. Captain Brady wasn't entirely comfortable with that. SWAT teams planned everything meticulously. They factored in what could go wrong and how they'd deal with it. But these people from Gamlin played by a very different book. And he hadn't read it. By the time they reached Goodwin, snow was beginning to fall quite heavily.

It was McClure who broke the silence. 'If the Johnson house is on the other side of the river, why are we going down this side?'

'The only bridge is at Fort Fairfield,' said Ravenhart. 'It's also pretty exposed round the house and we can park up out of sight in the town.'

'So how are you getting us in there?'

Ravenhart tapped his case. 'I have a shield device. It blocks us from view.' He decided not to tell them about its limitations.

Once on the outskirts of Fort Fairfield, Brady told the driver to turn off the main road along the river and cut through the back streets. They pulled off into Community Centre Drive and parked the truck away behind some buildings. The team disgorged and found themselves ankle deep in snow. It was still coming down.

'Could have done without this,' muttered Brady.

The three SWAT boys were busy strapping on weapons and body armour. Rotsko, McClure, Carson and Loey checked their guns and slipped on coats and parkas, pulling them up tight around their necks to keep out the snow and cold. Ravenhart, unmoved by the temperature, stood with his long coat open and flapping in the gentle wind. In one hand he carried his small brown leather case. McClure burst out laughing.

'What's the joke?' asked Rotsko.

'He looks like a lost salesman from New York.'

They all laughed. Ravenhart regarded them, his black eyes showing no emotion. He waited a beat then said, 'We best get going.' He turned round and walked away towards Elm Street which led up to the river.

McClure shrugged his shoulders. 'Do they do humour on Gamlin?' he asked no-one in particular and set off after him. Rotsko pulled up alongside

Ravenhart, struggling to fit in with his long loping stride.

'We *are* going to do this.'

Ravenhart was silent for several minutes. 'If it was just me and Crolin I would be fine with that. We hunters work on our own. I'm not sure about all this team stuff.'

'But it isn't just you and Crolin. He has two others who've been parachuted in. If they're here that is.'

'Oh, they'll be here.'

'And?'

'And this is likely to happen very fast Rotsko. I can't watch everybody. If I take my eye off Crolin's game this will go wrong.'

'What are you saying?'

'I'm saying people back there need to think and act fast when it kicks off.'

It was Rotsko's turn to walk along in silence. The eight of them looked out of place striding down a Fort Fairfield back road. Three of them obviously armed. But the weather was keeping people indoors. Ravenhart suddenly stopped and faced Rotsko. The others had fallen behind.

'What is it?'

'You know, not everyone is going to survive this.'

The police chief looked over Ravenhart's shoulder, watching the snow gathering on rooftops. He nodded. 'Let's just do our best Ravenhart.' They carried on walking.

'He's here.'

'What?' said Harrigan.

'The hunter. He's here. I can sense him,' said Crolin. The three of them were settled on the ground among the trees by the river.

'Surely three of us can take out one hunter? Even Ravenhart,' said Brynchek.

'Don't underestimate him for a moment. He is dangerous and he is capable of taking out three,' said Crolin. 'But not us,' he said almost to himself. 'Not us.'

He sunk deep into thought. After 200 years of vengeance missions, one simple trip to take out two victims had suddenly turned into a pivotal confrontation. This wasn't just about honour anymore; the continuing, unending quest for revenge on the descendants of those who had all but destroyed his family thousands of years ago. This was about a power struggle that was exploding back on Gamlin. So much more was at stake. Crolin couldn't get this wrong. Not here. Not now in some snowbound community up in North Maine. He thought long and hard. Trying to put himself in Ravenhart's place. The problem with that was Ravenhart was unpredictable. That's what made him so good. Crolin was going to have to come up with some sort of plan. He looked across at Harrigan and Brynchek, nodding his head slowly as a glimmer of an idea shaped itself in his mind.

Ravenhart called a halt at the edge of the bridge. 'Wait here a moment. Brady and Rotsko come with me.'

Visibility was closing in as the snow thickened. They reached the other side and then cut down right towards the edge of the river. It looked like a strip of cold steel sliding away under the bridge. Ravenhart crouched. 'I need you to take a good look at what we've got here.'

Brady edged forward to a small rise, fetched some binoculars out of his jacket pocket and scanned the area. The house was drifting in and out of view as the snow swirled. He could make out the shed on their side of the house, but nothing was moving. Even the river was quiet in that silent world. He tracked back to Ravenhart and Rotsko.

'It's all very open ground. No cover apart from those trees and shrubs further along the river here. No sign of anyone either.'

'They're here. I can tell you that much,' said Ravenhart. The two men looked at him. Ravenhart just shrugged his shoulders. 'I think you call it a sixth sense. Crolin will also know that I'm here so it evens things out a little on that front.'

'So how we going to play this?' asked Rotsko.

'We're going to have to split the team up as planned and go in as two groups, but there will be a problem.'

'And what problem is that?' asked Brady.

'I can only keep one group under cover. The

shield only hides those who are grouped up with the user.'

'Which will be you,' said Rotsko.

'Actually no.' It took both men by surprise. 'Crolin already knows I'm here, but he won't know about everyone else.'

'How come? What about all this *sensing* stuff.'

'That doesn't extend beyond Gamlin people, but I won't bore you with the biology of that just now. Rotsko, you will use the shield. I don't want Crolin to know about the back-up team. I need to keep that advantage in hand.'

'Makes sense,' said Brady.

'Right let's get back to the others.'

Crolin laid out his plan. 'Right this is what we do. Harrigan I want you in the house fast and grab hold of the woman, but don't harm her,' his voice was fierce. His eyes shone. 'I will deal with her. She's my honour killing. I won't be robbed again.'

The Aracanate just nodded.

'Brynchek I want you up in the gap between the side of the house and that small building and be ready to move the moment I say.'

'What are you doing?' he asked.

'That's my business. Just get going. Now!'

The pair slunk away towards the house and once out of Crolin's earshot Harrigan simply said, 'He's setting us up.'

'Yup, we're the bait to flush out Ravenhart, but I have no plans on being a victim.'

Harrigan grinned. 'Ok we split here. Stay sharp.'

Crolin watched them head towards the house, then made his way further along the river.

The team was standing in a semi-circle in front of Ravenhart. Fidgety and nervous. Not really knowing what awaited them. Aware they were totally in the hands of this slim strange man from another world who stood there — coat undone and flapping in the cold wind, long black hair and black eyes that gave absolutely no hint of what was going on behind them. In his hand he held what looked like a small TV remote control made out of platinum type metal. But it was no metal they'd ever come across.

'This is going to go off very fast so it's critical we each understand our part and play it out quickly,' said Ravenhart. 'This is the shield device.'

'That won't even cover my ...'

'Quiet McClure,' growled Rotsko.

'It will not work for all of us,' continued Ravenhart. 'Probably four will be best.'

'And the other three lucky ones going with you?' asked McClure.

'I won't be one of them. It will be Rotsko leading Carson, Loey and one your SWAT guys, Brady.'

'That'll be you, Waffin,' ordered Brady.

'The device is straightforward. Push this pad here and ....' Ravenhart disappeared.

'Shit!' It was McClure's expletive, the rest just stood there, mouths open. Ravenhart reappeared.

'The bastard is actually smiling,' said the detective.

'When the cloaking device is activated it casts a grey shadow on the ground. Stay within that and you'll be hidden from view. So when Rotsko moves, you move. And stay tight.' He handed it over to him.

'We'll be going up to the shed,' said Rotsko. 'Our primary goal is to secure the safety of the woman inside the house.'

Ravenhart turned to Brady. 'You, me, McClure and your other man are heading down river into the trees. We're after Crolin. He must be taken alive, no question. I have no problem with the other two being deconstructed.'

'What the fuck is deconstructed?'

'I think you call it killing them McClure.'

Chapter 15

THE snow hadn't let up. If anything it was getting heavier. It helped everybody and nobody. Seeing anything was beginning to get difficult. Rotsko called his group around him, looked at Ravenhart and then at the cloaking device in his hand.

'This pad here then?'

Ravenhart nodded. 'Right we'd better get going. Rotsko you move your team over the bridge first.'

Carson, Loey and one of the SWAT men gathered around Rotkso at the entrance to the bridge while the rest looked on. Rotsko hit the pad and all he was aware of was a grey circular shadow suddenly appearing on the ground around the team. As far as everyone else was concerned the four of them had vanished. 'I'll set the pace. I want one of you either side of me and one just behind. I'll keep it steady, just make sure you stay in the shadow.' Rotsko could feel his stomach muscles tense as he began to move off. He felt naked, exposed as they made their way across the bridge even though he knew they were all invisible. He wondered about the footprints they were leaving in the snow, but trusted that the poor visibility would save their skins.

The team pulled up just the other side. 'All ok with how this is going?' They nodded. 'We quit talking from here on out. No point being invisible then gabbing away, so silent communication please.' They trudged off across open ground towards the house.

McClure was getting fidgety. 'Time to go?'

'Give them another few minutes. I want them well clear before we enter the arena,' said Brady. They stood there for another few minutes stamping their feet in the cold then Ravenhart told them it was time to go.

He led them across the bridge and cut down to the trees and shrubs at the river's edge. He stopped, his senses bristling, knowing Crolin was out there somewhere.

'Let's move on.' Brady's voice cut through the tension. 'Weapons readied. McClure you watch right,

I'll take left.' He nodded to Ravenhart who led on to the wide expanse of open ground between them and the house.

Crolin was farther down the river bank, once again invisible and he watched the team make its way slowly up towards the house. He identified Ravenhart straightaway and gave a tight smile at the thought of finally taking down this iconic hunter. He was also comfortable with the odds. Sure that he, Brynchek and Harrigan could take down the team of four. They had surprise on their side after all. But even so Ravenhart's obvious approach set an alarm bell ringing quietly in the back of his mind.

Then everything started unravelling fast. A piercing scream from the house cut through the air followed by shots and shouts. Rotsko's team had almost arrived at the shed by the side of the house when everything cut loose. As the woman started screaming Brynchek ran towards the back door of the house and cannoned into the invisible police chief. The shock delayed any reaction — and that cost the Arcanate his life as Carson and Loey let loose a fusillade of shots into him.

Ravenhart and the others quickly arrived on the scene after running up the hill to the house. 'What the fuck's happened?' asked Brady.

'No idea,' said Rotsko. 'Something's gone off inside and this guy came belting round the corner but obviously wasn't aware we were here.'

Ravenhart checked that Brynchek was dead; muttered something under his breath. 'Rotsko take your guys in through the back door we'll go in at the front. Move it!'

The front door on the porch opened into a sitting room and the back door opened into the kitchen. They were directly in line with each other, a small corridor linking the two rooms. Both doors splintered virtually simultaneously as the teams crashed through them. Harrigan was against one wall in the front room, his arm around the woman's neck. He yanked the Johnson girl hard against his chest, trying to use her as a shield. His weapon ready.

The teams had instantly fanned out as they entered the house, but the corridor was a nasty pinch point and as Carson and Loey bunched up heading into the sitting room Harrigan swung round and fired. The officers were engulfed in a red beam which surged and flickered around them. They died not knowing how.

Brady was behind them and dropped to one knee his Heckler levelled at Harrigan, but he had no way of hitting him. At that point though, the Arcanate, had turned away from Ravenhart who moved in a blur, rammed his weapon against Harrigan's neck and fired. A red beam flared and he dropped to the floor. The woman let out a gasping sob as she collapsed.

For a split second silence filled the small room.

Rotsko lifted the woman to her feet. 'You okay Lorraine?' She nodded her head. 'This is Lorraine Banahan everyone. She's a cop. We moved Sally Jackson's daughter to a safe house as we didn't want Crolin getting near her, but we did need a woman at home here.'

'Jesus what happened to Carson and Loey,' said McClure as he walked towards their bodies. 'There's no fucking injuries to them, how the fuck can they be dead?'

'The weapons deconstruct the nervous system and effectively stop all brain activity. It's not as messy as your methods.'

McClure turned on Ravenhart: 'What's THAT supposed to mean?' He grabbed him by the lapels and slammed him against the wall. 'Is that supposed to fucking help? Is it?'

The Gamlin looked at him, his black eyes unreadable.

'McClure!' Rotsko's voice cut through like ice. The detective slumped, energy drained out of him. His grip on Ravenhart's coat relaxed.

'It's just the shock,' said Rotsko.

Ravenhart nodded. McClure finally let Ravenhart go. 'Sorry man, it's just that ....' He waved his arm at the scene.

Ravenhart lightly touch McClure's shoulder. 'I do understand McClure.'

The detective sucked in a deep breath and blew out hard. 'Yeah.'

'Where's Crolin.' Brady's question silenced everyone. A chill ran through the room.

'Oh he's not far away,' said Ravenhart. 'He used the other two as decoys to trap us in here, probably hoping to take down those around me and leave me isolated. His problem is that because of the shield he didn't realise how many of us there are. He's also going to be pretty upset when he realises the Jackson girl isn't here.'

'So what's our plan?' asked Brady.

'We can't stay in here,' said Rotsko, 'We're too bunched up.'

'Agreed,' said Brady.

'We could use the shield to get out without him seeing us,' suggested McClure.

'That'd work,' added Rotsko. 'Ravenhart? You hearing all this?'

The hunter motioned for them to be quiet. 'He's just outside,' he whispered.

McClure started saying: 'How do...' before Rotsko dug him in the ribs.

Ravenhart indicated that people should move against a wall at the back of the lounge and then moved into the middle of the room. He stood still, head slightly on one side as if listening for something. Suddenly he dropped to a crouch and fired. A green beam shot from his weapon, surging away through a window to his left. Behind him there was a terrible cracking and part of the house's wooden wall split open as if cleaved by an axe; splinters flying everywhere.

Crolin's vicious, black spike lanced through the narrow gap, slashing the air. It vanished again and another splintering crash saw his armoured lizard head smashing a large hole in the side of the building. His long tongue flicked in and out; the yellow eyes almost hypnotic as they gazed at Ravenhart. Quick as lightning the tail lashed back into the room, but this time towards the group huddled in a corner. It caught Corrigan in his leg. He screamed in pain.

Crolin roared as beams from Ravenhart's weapon hit the wall by his head. He pulled away out of the gap. They could still hear him roaring outside. And then it went quiet again.

'Corrigan's in a lot of pain,' said Rotsko.

Ravenhart reached inside his coat, brought a syringe. 'For emergencies.' He bent down over the

SWAT man, placed the device against his leg and injected the antidote. 'He'll be okay. We need to get out of here.'

'Crolin will be waiting for us,' said McClure.

'I'm banking on that.' Ravenhart's eyes were hard.

Rotsko held up the shield control. 'Might this be some use?'

Crolin was consumed with rage. And that was a bad thing. This partial loss of self-control left him locked down in shapeshift form and unable to fade into the background. What he did know was that the hunter certainly didn't intend to kill him. The red beam was a killer, the green beam was for stun. For the first time Crolin had the nagging feeling he was no longer in control of events. He gazed at the house, working out what to do next. Realising that being out in the open was a distinct disadvantage, Crolin started scuttling towards the back door of the house. As he got there Ravenhart emerged.

The spike lashed out, but found only thin air as

Ravenhart rolled away. He levelled his weapon but was forced to move quickly as the spike again jabbed towards him. This time Crolin grabbed at him with a pincer, caught him round the neck and jerked the hunter up in the air. Poison was blooming on the tip of Crolin's tail spike.

Behind him the rest of the team, hidden by the shield, launched a hail of bullets. Crolin roared and spun round. It was all Ravenhart needed as he brought up his weapon and fired a long burst of green energy which swarmed all over the Arcanate. The scream from Crolin was primeval. Ravenhart dropped like a stone to the ground and everyone else scattered as the tail spike lashed wildly around in the air. The hues of green shimmered around the lizard-like creature. Ravenhart fired again and in an instant the beast vanished leaving Crolin writhing on the floor. The hunter hadn't finished yet, flicked a switch on his weapon and fired once more. This time blue beams swirled around Crolin until he could no longer move.

Ravenhart stood up and pocketed his weapon as the team gathered round him. They were all staring at Crolin.

'That's it,' said Ravenhart.

'That's it? That's it? Is that all you can say? That's it?' said McClure waving his hand vaguely around the scene.

'Well, I have Crolin. What more is there to say?' Ravenhart's black eyes were impassive.

'What's the equivalent of a high five on Gamlin?'

'Sorry?'

'Never mind. Good job man, but I bet you're glad we had you covered there eh?'

'I was banking on it,' said Ravenhart.

'Brady, I need my pack from the truck.'

'Sure,' said the SWAT captain. 'Sieven, go get the man his case.' The SWAT man set off while the rest stood over the inert form of Crolin, the blue rings pulsing round his body.

'That sure is neat,' said McClure. 'Bit more efficient than cuffs wouldn't you say chief?'

Rotsko nodded.

'Wouldn't have a spare pair of those I guess?'

Ravenhart chuckled and shook his head

without comment. Sieven returned and handed the small, tan leather case to the hunter. He opened it and took out the gatetrap.

'Time I was going people. Got to get Crolin back and put down a rebellion.'

'Steady man, you're heading towards humour country,' said McClure. Ravenhart flashed a quick smile and activated the gate. 'Thanks for your help all.'

A deep thrumming sound rose to a whine. Five violet beams then hovered in the air. Ravenhart hauled Crolin up, put him across his shoulder and stepped through the beams. And they were gone.

'Sentimental bastard wasn't he. That goodbye almost choked me up,' said McClure. 'So how do we explain this mess chief?'

'Pretty straightforward if you think about it McClure,' said Rotsko. 'We cornered the guy here, rescued the woman, but he got away in all this snow and over into New Brunswick. They can hunt him down.'

'And how do we explain Ravenhart?'

'Never heard of him McClure. Never heard of

him.' Rotsko turned and trudged off through the snow towards the bridge.

This book was edited and published with love and care by

Strawberry Pirate Ltd.

http://www.strawberrypirate.com